VIKING UNBOUND

VIKING UNBOUND

THE TRIAD SERIES, BOOK 3

KATE PEARCE

PROLOGUE

YORK, ENGLAND 970. A.D.

"We're not going to survive this time, brother." Aki's voice echoed around the dark cavern as they ran. "Someone betrayed us."

"I know that," Einarr snarled. "And, by the Gods, he will regret it."

"If we live."

Einarr took another turn and continued downward, the sound of underground water now in front of him. "We'll live." He slowed his step, as the light ahead grew stronger.

"By running away like cowards?" Aki was breathing hard. "They've blocked the entrance to this cave. All they have to do is come after us. We'll be easy prey."

"We're not running away." The eerie white light bounced off Einarr's shield and axe. The power of his ancestors surged within him and answered the call of the ancient magic. "Grandfather told me about this place. He said that if I ever needed an escape, the waterfall would provide one."

Aki gasped as they stepped into a huge cavern where water tumbled in a frothing white mass down from the farthest black rock formation.

"There's a way out?" Aki had to yell to be heard.

Einarr reached behind him and grasped Aki's arm ring, sending a wave of power that pushed his words directly into his twin brother's head.

"Aye. Behind the waterfall. We just have to walk through to the other side." Einarr took a step forward, one hand on his axe. *"Be careful. It's slippery."*

Aki followed him as the well-worn path climbed steadily until they reached a smooth stone platform that seemed to disappear directly inside the roar of the white-flecked water. Einarr set down his shield and his brother did the same.

"Hold onto my cloak." Einarr said.

"I'm not a babe in arms," Aki complained, but obeyed him anyway. "May Odin protect us."

As Einarr inched forward, everything inside him slowed and coalesced into a burning hot sensation in his fingertips. He reached out his hand and the water turned to steam, lifting the curtain to show him the continuing path and a narrow cavern behind the falls. He kept moving and the waterfall closed behind them leaving an eerie screaming silence that made him want to shove his fingers in his ears and shriek like a frightened child.

The noise rose until the rocks were vibrating, and all the hair on his body stood upright like an animal at bay. Sparks flew from his outstretched fingertips ricocheting off the walls and slicing through the water like the sharpest dagger cuts.

"Einarr!"

He looked back and Aki screamed as the water turned inward and coalesced into ice. Then he knew no more.

1

TRIOS SPACE AGENCY SHIP QZ41 - TRIOS
SYSTEM 229995.

"So what we have here, Tecky is a bona fide prehistoric popsicle?"

"Not quite *prehistoric*, but certainly ancient." Frey glanced over at the ship's captain and tried to smile. "My name's Frey, Captain Travis, not Tecky."

He held open a door and locked it behind her with yet another security code. "I know what your name is. We call all the science officers Tecky. It makes things easier to remember as you come and go so fast."

"I suppose that makes sense."

She tried to sound calm and approachable. It was her first job, and she didn't want to give the wrong impression. The FREN organization, the Federal Research Environmental Nation, employed all the scientists on Trios System ships, and she desperately wanted to be one of them for more than just her probationary year. Unfortunately, from what she'd seen so far, the crew on this particular ship was rather casual about rules and regulations and found her insistence on following protocol rather amusing.

"I've been specially trained to keep an eye on this cargo, Captain."

"Why, what do they think is going to happen?" Travis laughed, the sound bouncing off the spherical metal walls. "Hopefully that thing is frozen solid."

"The ice is untouched. And that's how it will remain until we put down on Alpha Station Three."

Travis unlocked the last door and handed her the secure passkey. The temperature dropped as they approached the glass-viewing screen. Frey flipped the lights on.

"Well, Holy Magnet, he looks like a real live man, doesn't he?" Travis whistled. "Like he was freeze-framed from a holo-image rather than really frozen. Do you guys know how it happened?"

"We're not quite sure. It looks as though he and the other specimen were encased in ice so suddenly that they were preserved intact."

"When do you reckon that was?"

"About four thousand Earth years ago."

Travis whistled again. "Who found them?"

"Part of an old copper mine gave way near the ancient city of York and revealed the caverns beneath the city. The Earth scientists believe the males might be of Viking origin."

"You're kidding," Travis leaned in on the glass and shaded his eyes with his hand. "Looks like the guy has some kind of axe."

"You're correct, captain. The other specimen on your sister ship is holding a sword or a bow. We're not quite sure what it is yet."

"So they're going to defrost them on Alpha Three like frozen pigcow?"

"It's a bit more technical than that, but I suppose it is a similar process."

"We could stick him in our FoodPro and see if that would work. We'd save billions for the Trios Space Agency."

Frey smiled tightly again as the ship's captain laughed at his own joke and left her to survey her frozen science project. Travis was a confident man and despite first impressions seemed efficient, which was why she supposed he'd been chosen to carry such a precious cargo.

She went to switch the lights off and then lingered, one hand flat on the glass. Every time she looked at the Viking she noticed more details, the dark stubble on the warrior's chin, the heavy rings on his fingers and the arm bands with the Nordic writing and runes no one had gotten close enough to yet to decipher.

But soon they would. Frey could only hope she'd be allowed to stay and watch the great thawing out. The Alpha Three scientists were renowned for rediscovering and reintroducing lost species to their native environments. As far as she knew, no one had ever tried to revive two ancient Vikings…

With a quick look behind her, she let herself into the holding cell. Despite what she'd said to the captain, the FREN team had already penetrated the ice around the male more than once. Four tiny microscopic probes had been inserted. She was the only one onboard with the necessary clearance to read and monitor those probes.

The block of ice stood about three meters high and a meter wide on a plinth that provided power and cooling jets to keep the ice from melting or deteriorating further. This close, the ice was almost clear. Sometimes, it felt like the warrior's eyes were following her around as she worked, but they were still closed tight. She wondered what his eye color would be when he finally regained consciousness, and what he would make of the world he'd woken up in. She had to assume it would be terrifyingly unfamiliar.

She checked the sensors. Everything registered a big fat zero, which was just fine with her. It was quite a responsibility, but she was more than up for it. She'd also been given detailed instructions about what to do in any kind of emergency situation and how her primary function was to save the ice warrior at all costs. Not that anything would go wrong. The small crew flew this route at least twice an Earth month, and there was nothing hostile on the way to Alpha Station Three.

"Tecky, you receiving me?"

She didn't need to use her com to hear her fellow Pavlovan. They were both telepaths. Frey hadn't made many close friends during her year on Earth. She'd either been studying too hard, or been too reserved to get into the whole college culture. As a result, she valued having someone around on the ship she could talk to so easily. *"Yes, First Officer Slavin."*

"Come and strap yourself in, we're about to depart."

Frey blew a scandalous kiss to her important cargo, and after securely locking the series of doors, made her way to the bridge where the other members of the crew were already seated.

Slavin smiled as Frey went by her seat. "All secure down there?"

"Yes, thanks."

"We're not anticipating any problems on this flight. It will take about five cycles. We'll sleep through most of it."

"Good." Frey settled more comfortably in the deep padded seat and studied the blackness of space. There was so frakking much of it that sometimes it scared her. She liked her world to be ordered and controllable and…why the *heeze* had she ever wanted to work for an intergalactic corporation?

During the first space jumps, they'd all be immobilized in a semiconscious state as the ship followed its pre-programmed course and brought them closer to where they needed to be. The chairs acted like life support, monitoring body signs, offering the necessary nutrition and sending all pertinent information back to Earth and the various planets involved in case of emergency.

"There is one interesting thing happening out there," Slavin added. "We're expecting an up-close and personal look at a massive eclipse."

"Oh, that's right! Five planets are lining up." Frey grinned. "Being a science geek, I'm ridiculously excited about this."

"Alpha Station Three is between the last two of the aligning planets, Thor and Odin."

"Then my Norseman will appreciate that."

Slavin raised her eyebrows. "Your Norseman?"

Frey pointed down at the hold. "The frozen guy. Thor and Odin are Viking gods."

"Then it's a shame he won't be awake to see it."

"Maybe I'll open up the viewing screens in the lab so that he can get a peek at it. I'll probably have to view most of it from there anyway to catch and interpret the data stream for TSA and FREN."

"Lucky old you."

Frey relaxed as the thrusters started to rumble, and Slavin turned her attention to piloting the ship out of the dock and into open space. Sensors emerged from the arms and back of the chair and coiled themselves around Frey as the big engines kicked in and they set up for their first jump.

Now all she had to do was sit back and enjoy the ride.

2

SOMETHING CALLED TO HIM...

Something he couldn't see, but could sense deep within, like the pounding of his heart, the suck of air into his lungs or the throb of his cock...

Did he want to respond to that nameless urging? He'd tried before, but had given up in despair, his power too weak to force himself out of his stupor.

But this was more visceral. More of a demand, as if something gripped his heart and threatened to rip it from his chest while it was still beating... Had Odin finally released him from his hell with the promise of a fight to the death and the ultimate glory of a seat in Valhalla?

Light.

There.

The smallest pinprick. A blackish glow that infiltrated his skull like a red-hot wire or the tang of a bloodied lip. It burrowed inside him and shattered into a thousand pieces. He screamed in agony.

"Wow."

Frey knew she was talking to herself, but she didn't care. There was no one else in the lab aside from the unmoving slab of frozen Viking. So, she talked to him when no one was around. What was wrong with that? Okay, she dreamed about him too, but those images were too erotic to think about while she was working.

She'd opened the viewing screens on the lower deck so that she could get a good look at the eclipse, which was lining up to be spectacular. Four of the planets, including her home planet Pavlovan were now aligned, and the fifth would be engulfed fairly shortly. The reflected light made the planets glow blood red, like four various sized discs superimposed upon each other. The smallest planet, Thor, would slide into place within the next few minutes and then hold position for about the same length of time until the planets moved away from each other again.

Data streamed down from six screens in an endless torrent. Frey had no time to analyze it properly, which didn't sit well with her. Her role was to make sure all the cameras and readers were functioning and relaying the information back to the FREN and Pavlovan scientists who had never witnessed this particular phenomenon before.

First Officer Slavin had said that several nations were also monitoring the eclipse. She had offered to stay on the bridge for the nightshift just to watch it happen. Frey thought seeing it through the sealed windows of the space ship was way more interesting than just staring at the screens. As far as Frey knew, there was no danger in looking directly at the alignment through the thick protection of TecGlass, so she was soaking up every second.

After another quick check of the screens, she turned back to the window, holding her breath as the planet Thor finally slid into place right in the center of the slightly bigger Odin. Waves of redness seemed to undulate from the five planets making Frey blink.

"That's *awesome*," she whispered suddenly aware of what that overused word really meant.

A flash on one of the monitors made her look up as all the screens suddenly went haywire.

Frey tried to make sense of the gibberish now running on the screens, which flashed on and off. With a sudden explosion of color, the image disappeared leaving all the screens black.

"Holy *heeze*," Frey muttered as she frantically pushed every button she could find. "What happened?"

"Are you okay down there?"

"Yeah, but the data stream just collapsed. Is everything okay with the ship, Slavin?"

"Nope, all screens blacked out here and the coms. Life support is fully functioning though."

"Frak," Frey muttered as the screens flashed from black to red and back again. *"Do you need to wake the captain?"*

"I'll—" Slavin's breath hissed out. *"Oh, thank the Gods, we're back online. I'm going to run some tests. You okay down there?"*

Frey blinked as her screens stayed red, and random columns of figures cascaded downward like an uncontrollable waterfall.

"I'm registering something. I'm not quite sure what it is." She leaned closer to the screen and squinted against the fierceness of the red. *"It looks like gibberish and it's certainly not English. Hieroglyphics maybe? Runes?"*

The six screens flashed simultaneously and Frey instinctively shut her eyes. When she opened them again the data stream had returned to normal.

"Tecky? Frey? Are you still there?"

She fumbled to sit upright, mortally embarrassed that she'd somehow ended up under her desk like a three year old. *"I'm fine, Slavin. It just got a bit bright in here. Everything's back to normal now."*

"Good." Slavin hesitated. *"You sound a bit shaken. Do you want me to send security down?"*

"No, I'm good, I really am." Frey shook herself and stood up, smoothing down her tightly tied back hair. She tried to appear like the competent officer she was. *"I have to check on my cargo."*

She picked up the specially tuned recorder the FREN rep had given her and turned toward the cold storage zone. Even through the glass, she could still see the block of ice and the Viking encased inside. Red light reflecting off the eclipse outside gave the ice a rosy pink glow with a smattering of dancing crimson lights.

Frey unlocked the security door and went in. She didn't realize she was holding her breath until it whooshed out in a little cloud of heated air. She put a tentative hand on the ice. It was frozen hard and the cooling jets beneath it still functioned perfectly.

Turning on the recorder, she walked around the block of ice, giving the receptors time to pick up all four probes. The signal beeped and registered another zero, and Frey sent a prayer up to the Pavlovan heavens. She'd go through the complete records tomorrow, after she'd reported the fault to her superiors back at FREN. They'd probably already noticed there was a break in transmission, but there was a slight delay in receiving information, so she didn't expect to hear back from them right away. It gave her plenty of time to analyze the problem and send them a complete report herself.

A flash of light glinted off the ice, and she stared back through the glass into her empty lab where the screens were functioning perfectly and beyond her desk to the still amazing sight of the aligned planets. A soft sigh echoed around the enclosed space and the ice creaked and groaned.

The recorder in her hand buzzed. She looked down at it and

then further down to the metallic floor where something red glinted against the corner of the ice block. Frey crouched down and studied the gleaming red droplet, laughing with stupid relief as she realized it was just a reflection of the eclipse. For a second, it had looked more like a solid gemstone.

Her smile dimmed. Her back was now blocking the colors of the eclipse and yet the red was still there…Tentatively she leaned forward and touched the droplet. It adhered to her skin, a perfect red globe and she brought it closer to her face and sniffed it, wondering at the coppery smell. Was one of the probes within the ice malfunctioning or even worse, rusting? It seemed unlikely, but she would mention it on her next report.

Even as she stared at the red droplet it started to lose its shape. She flicked her finger and jumped as a sharp pain pieced her skin.

"Ouch! What the frak was that?" She flinched as a bead of her own blood now bloomed in the exact same place as the red droplet had been. Instinctively, she brought her finger to her mouth and sucked on it.

"Eew, no that was stupid!"

She flicked her fingers, and holding her hand up and away from herself went through the process of relocking the security doors until she was safety back in the lab and able to raid the medical kit for a disinfectant spray to close the wound. She should have been wearing gloves before she touched the ice or even went near it. In her haste to check that the Viking was still okay, she'd forgotten procedure and ended up doing something monumentally stupid.

God knows what she could've done in there, adding her blood to the controlled atmosphere around the ice. She was a complete idiot. It was *so* not like her to do something so unprofessional.

"Everything okay down there, Tecky?" Slavin came on the com.

"Yes, everything's fine. No change in our cargo, and all my screens are working perfectly now."

"Good, I don't think there is any point in waking the whole crew up over this. We'll mention what happened to the captain at the handover in the morning, okay?"

"Fine by me."

"Then I'll see you up here on the bridge in three hours."

"Will do." Frey signed off and put away the medical kit. She'd give her report to the captain in the morning as to the effect of the eclipse on her sensors and instruments, but she wasn't going to mention her bleeding finger. Unfortunately, that information would be available for FREN to view on their specially installed cameras in the hold, which meant she might be about to lose her job.

With a groan she glared at her throbbing finger. So much for her long career as a Science Officer roaming the galaxies for FREN and TSA. She'd blown it. As soon as she got to Alpha Three she'd be fired.

She probably wouldn't even be allowed to stay long enough to see what happened to the Viking, and without FREN security clearance she probably never would find out if he survived... And that was unacceptable. She already felt a deep connection with him that unsettled her. Maybe it was that being associated with his reemergence into the world would help her scientific career, but it felt so much more...as if she was somehow supposed to defend him against everyone and every thing.

There was no point trying to hide what she'd done. Perhaps her honesty would work in her favor and they'd simply demote her rather than letting her go.

"Yeah, right." Frey muttered. "FREN is so well known for its compassion."

She settled back in her seat and started to compose her report and, just in case, her resignation.

THE BUZZ of her com in her ear woke her and she sat up, aware that she'd fallen asleep at her desk analyzing data and that her hair was stuck to her face with what was either tears or drool. Whatever it was, she was glad there wasn't any vidscreen action. She hated looking less than immaculate.

"Tecky? We need you up here pronto."

"Yes, Captain."

She wished she had time to change but did the best she could to smooth down her hair and freshen up. She took the elevator to the bridge and arrived to find the whole crew already there.

"I hear there were some problems last night." Travis nodded to Frey to sit down and then pointed at Slavin. "What happened?"

"There was a small blip in our power when the eclipse reached its magnitude. I checked with Tecky in the lab to see if she was okay. Just as I was doing that all my systems returned to normal." Slavin consulted her handtech unit. "I've tested all systems and security classifications and there is no damage or indication why the outage occurred."

"Life support wasn't affected?"

"No Captain, just the screens on the bridge, which became nonfunctional for about thirty clicks."

"What about the navigational functions of the ship?"

"Unimpaired. It was as if the data streams were interrupted for a few seconds." Slavin shrugged. "I wondered if the perfect alignment of the eclipse had something to do with it, but as we've no record of this planetary event happening before, I don't have any data to back up my theory."

Captain Travis studied the data Slavin handed him. "Carry on with your tests and relay everything you're doing back to FREN, Earth and Pavlovan. They might have additional information for us. Until we hear anything different, we'll proceed as planned to Alpha Three."

"Yes, sir." Slavin nodded.

Frey tensed as the captain turned to her.

"Everything okay with your cargo, Tecky?"

"My screens went off for a few seconds, but there was no damage to the ice or the Viking that I could see. I've also written a report for FREN if you wish to read it."

Travis nodded. "Hell no, that's fine. Just make sure you send a copy along with Slavin's and any extra data you gathered when you checked your systems to FREN and every other damn agency that will insist on seeing it."

"Yes, sir." Frey sank back into her chair aware that Slavin was watching her closely. She made sure her telepathic shields were as high as she could before rising to her feet and nodding at the other crew members.

"I'm going to get something to eat. Is anyone coming?" Frey asked in her most cheerful *I have nothing to hide* voice.

"I'll come."

Slavin joined her in the elevator, her blond hair neatly tied back in a ponytail, her expression concerned.

"What's wrong?"

"Why should anything be wrong?" Frey asked.

"Because before you shoved your shields up, I sensed that you weren't telling the captain the entire truth. Is everything okay with your cargo?"

"He's fine. It's just that I forgot to put my gloves on last night and touched the ice barehanded. I'm worried I might have contaminated the space."

"The Viking's still frozen stiff, right?"

"Yeah he is."

The doors of the elevator opened on the mess level. *"Then you should be okay."*

Frey followed Slavin out of the elevator. *"You don't know*

FREN. They are really strict about proper procedure, and I'm a science officer. I should have remembered to keep the atmosphere pollutant free."

"It was an emergency situation. *You did your best."* Slavin said firmly. She pushed open the mess hall door. "Now come and get something to eat."

3

IT WAS LATE, BUT FREY WAS DETERMINED TO FINISH CHECKING through every bit of information that had accrued during the eclipse. She'd pinpointed the exact Earth second when the systems had attempted to crash. It had only been about one hundred and thirty seconds of lost power, but she still had no idea what had caused it.

Glancing up, she studied the five planets that had now moved away from each other. Appearances in space were deceptive. They still had quite a way to go before they reached the research station on Alpha Three, which was between two of the moons. She sighed and took another sip of her coffee, one of the few things she had really appreciated about her stint on Earth.

If by some chance she kept her job and got to witness the defrosting process, she was then due two months of leave on Pavlovan. Her family intended to take her to the temple to meet the Oracle and see if she would reveal at least one of Frey's chosen mates.

Frey finished the coffee in one gulp. She'd managed to avoid going to the temple on her last visit, but she couldn't miss it again. Despite her mother's checkered history with her mates, she would be upset if Frey didn't go. At twenty-five, she was quite old enough to find out what the future had in store for her —even if that meant agreeing to meet an unknown mate or two.

Her acquaintances on Earth had been horrified at the idea of having one's life partners chosen for you. Frey knew it worked and that partnerships on Pavlovan rarely broke up. Her parents had struggled, and her father had abandoned them, but two of her siblings were very happily mated and she expected to be the same. In fact, she wouldn't allow the outcome to be any different. A nice, dull Pavlovan male was all she wanted. No fireworks, no drama and no running off to find himself in the jungles of the north in Pavlovan.

Boring, safe, predictable mates just like her…

"Frey?"

"Hey." She turned to see Slavin in the doorway and beckoned her to come in. "I'm just going over the data again to see if I can make any more sense of it."

"Any luck?"

"Not so far."

Slavin helped herself to coffee and perched on the side of Frey's desk. "Any repercussions from FREN yet?"

"Not so far. I assume they are behind on data collection, and communications at this distance are spotty even for them."

"Thank goodness." Slavin grinned at her and toasted her with her mug of coffee. "Maybe they won't see you touch the ice at all."

"I'm pretty sure they will. They have their own cameras set up in the inner cell. I can't believe that I was so stupid. It's not like me. I'm notorious for checking everything twenty times." Frey topped off her mug of coffee. "If they let me complete the mission, I'm due home to Pavlovan for leave."

"Me too," Slavin grimaced. "My parents want me to meet my mate."

"You already have one?"

"No, they're going to haul me in front of the Oracle."

"Sounds just like my two mothers."

They shared a smile and then Slavin's com bleeped and she set her mug down on the desk. "Sorry, I've got to get back to the bridge."

"No worries. I have to finish up this report anyway." Frey stretched and groaned as Slavin patted her shoulder. "I'm not sure what I'm trying to prove here anymore—that it was an act of nature or that I was just incompetent."

"I'm sure FREN will decide that for you. I'll see you at breakfast."

"Will do."

Frey considered how much she'd come to like the tall blonde during their journey. She was smart, incisive and had a dry wit that Frey enjoyed immensely. Any Pavlovan should be glad to have her as his or her mate.

Her screen flashed red and the FREN logo appeared. Frey braced herself as the face of an unknown female appeared on the screen.

"Science Officer Frey. I am Director Mitzi Lahm."

"Director Lahm."

"We have received your data."

Frey stopped herself from babbling straight into an explanation and kept her expression serene.

"We have new orders for you."

She braced herself for dismissal, but saw instead a new file icon appear at the bottom of the screen.

"Read these, obey the instructions and then destroy them using FREN code TRZ9Y."

"Yes, Director. Thank you, ma'am"

Mitzi fixed her with a blistering gaze. "We will be discussing your unscientific conduct when you reach Alpha Three."

"Yes, Director."

"Over and out."

Trying not to dissolve into a small puddle of relief at not being instantly dismissed, Frey opened the orders file and considered the few short sentences. She grabbed her FREN recorder, and as requested, manually input the series of codes from the file into the database.

When the recorder beeped, she got down from her stool and unlocked the exterior and interior doors into the Viking's holding cell. She wrinkled her nose as she stepped into the final space. It felt warmer than it had yesterday. She automatically checked the temperature unit on the wall and the ice for signs of degradation but could see nothing unusual.

Except... she leaned closer to the ice, her breath misting on it. The Viking looked clearer today, and that was not possible. She could see the shaved sides of his head and the runes tattooed there, the thick sweep of long black hair hanging halfway down his back. Hardly daring to breathe, she pointed the recorder at the ice and waited for the four sensors to respond to the new commands as she circled the raised block.

"Hjálpa mér."

Frey went still. The telepathic thought was faint, the voice unfamiliar and the language unknown. She was fairly certain that apart from Slavin, there wasn't another Pavlovan on the ship, so who was projecting thoughts to her?

The sensors beeped and she jumped and looked down at the screen. *Heeze*, what was going on now? There were numbers where there should've been zeroes.

After one quick glance at the ice, she went back to the lab and entered her secure codes for FREN. It took but a click to feed the new data back to the director. She waited tensely in her seat, but there was no reply. What the hell was she supposed to do now?

Curiosity drove her back to the ice and the Viking within. Even in the time that she'd been away, the ice was even clearer. Three of the probes were now visible. She squinted closely at the still figure and finally detected the fourth device, which seemed to have been placed right against the Viking's skull.

It was winking red like a ruby, reminding her of the droplet of red blood she'd collected on her finger. Was that where the blood had come from? Dread settled low in her gut and she backed against the door.

"Slavin? Can you come down here?"

"Is it important?"

"I think it might be." Frey hesitated. *"Did you pick up any telepathic activity earlier?"*

"Apart from you? No, why?"

"Then you really should get down here. I'm...scared."

"Hang in there. I'm calling security."

Frey stayed where she was blocking the exit. She had the stupid sense that if she left the space the Viking might follow her…

Within minutes, Slavin appeared on the other side of the glass with the head of security, a competent male called Brown.

His voice sounded in her com. "What's wrong, Tecky?"

"The sensor readings have changed on the ice. It's warming up. I've reset the temperature controls twice, but nothing seems to make any difference."

"Are you trapped in there?"

"No, I just wanted someone with me when I tried to get out."

He nodded through the glass at her. "Then go ahead. I'll cover you and lock the door the second you're through it."

"You can't lock this door. I'm the only one who has the security clearance to do it."

"Then get out of there damn fast and lock it behind you."

"Okay."

She felt behind her for the passcode panel and trying not to take one eye off the ice block, tapped in her security code. The door unlocked and she whisked herself out of it and slammed it behind her. Her fingers shook as she recoded the door.

Brown studied her. "You all right, Tecky?"

"Not really. If this block of ice is melting, we're going to have a defrosting body on our hands, and FREN is going to freak out big time."

"Can you adjust the controls from here?" Slavin asked.

"Yes, I've tried it both ways, but nothing seems to be working."

"You've contacted FREN?"

"They contacted me and ordered me to input new codes. That's when everything started to go wrong. They haven't gotten back to me yet."

Slavin sighed. "Then I don't know what else we can do. I'll check in with the captain and see if there are any protocols I can adapt from the ship's main temperature controls to override or support what's in here. But this stuff was all introduced by FREN and made to their specific guidelines."

"Then let's hope they get back to me." Frey muttered.

HE COULD SENSE HER NOW, her thoughts jumbled and chaotic, and her fear palpable. That drew him to her and made him want to lick his lips in anticipation. Whatever she was, she was connected to him through his magic, and she would obey him. His eyelids twitched and he fought against the desire to force them open. Being encased in ice had taught him about patience and he would wait...there was no stopping his eventual emergence now; he knew it in his very being.

FREY COULDN'T SLEEP. She'd been dreaming about the Viking again, his black hair billowing in the breeze and his hand extended toward her. She'd gone to him and when they'd touched lips she'd moaned and unfortunately woken herself up. Her body throbbed a protest. It was the strangest sensation. She felt like she already knew the taste and texture of him intimately. She also had a sense that he needed her and was calling to her…

The captain had ordered security to guard the ice cell while she wasn't awake and to alert her to any significant changes, but her sense of need and dread refused to disperse. She didn't know why her nerves were jangling and her mind open to the slightest sound.

He *needed* her.

She sat up and pushed off the covers. Something was wrong and she was the only one who could fix it. FREN hadn't responded to her or to the captain so she was on her own.

If the Viking defrosted…

She ignored her shoes and went out into the narrow hallway that connected the crew quarters with the mess hall and administrative wing beyond. Above her were the more spacious cabins of the captain and those for official travelers. Below her, engines, cargo holds and the storage units. The subdued roar of the machines made the metal shudder and hum and the floor gently vibrate under her feet.

Ignoring the lure of the mess hall and the elevator, she climbed the spiral staircase up to her lab, her tension mounting along with her killer headache. She'd neglected to close the window shields. Her lab gleamed with red and yellow light reflecting from the exterior planets and their circling suns and stars.

A waft of freezing air made her stop and turn slowly toward the storage cell. She blinked hard at shards of broken glass and the slumped figure half-in and half-out of the first security door.

Grabbing both her weapon and her FREN recorder, she

dropped down to her knees and crawled slowly toward the fallen man. It was Prism one of the security guards. She felt for his pulse. His skin was frozen and she could see no other signs of life. Looking up at the security door she bit her lip. The glass looked like it had exploded from the inside...

Why the *heeze* weren't the alarms blaring? Why hadn't the rest of the security team appeared the instant one of their men went down? It was so damned quiet. Hardly daring to breathe, she eased past the man and the broken glass and focused her attention on the last of the security doors. The one she held the codes for.

"Gods, *no*," Frey whispered as she got a closer look at the mangled and distorted metal that had been practically ripped from its frame.

Knowing that she had to get even closer, she crawled forward and peered into the blackness within the holding cell. The motors hummed, keeping the air at well below freezing, but she had a sense that the Viking had forced his way out of there...

This wasn't good. This wasn't good at all.

She had to turn on a light and discover the truth. Her hands were shaking too much to make anything work. With a forlorn prayer to the Pavlovan Oracle and her Gods, she managed to illuminate the small screen of her FREN recorder and pointed it outward into the darkness.

The ice block had disappeared and so had its occupant.

Frey sat back on her ass and buried her face in her hands while she remembered how to breathe. She had to inform FREN that somehow their primitive Viking had self-defrosted and was now roaming the space ship obviously alive. And what the hell would he make of that? He could do untold damage and kill every one of them without even realizing what he'd done.

She tapped in the emergency code, added a short message and fumbled her way back into the main lab.

Her screen was already flashing an answer.

KEEP HIM ALIVE AT ALL COSTS. USE PROTOCOL 3ZE.

She stifled a hysterical giggle. That basically meant that she had control of the ship and the crew. She'd tried not to laugh when she'd been handed the secret protocols, knowing her chances of getting anyone to listen to her were fairly slim. But with a Viking marauder on the loose, would her companions change their minds?

First and foremost she had to find the Viking and communicate with him. Once that was achieved, she might have a chance to save both him and the crew. Rising to her feet, she rummaged in her desk for some additional items the FREN team had provided her with in case of an emergency and added them to her utility belt.

If she weren't allowed to kill him, she'd have to shut him down somehow. Her fingers steadied as she slid the buckle home and tightened the belt around her hips. A whisper of *something* touched her mind and she went still. It definitely wasn't Slavin's now familiar telepathic signature. Was it possible that Vikings in the first century A.D. on Earth had been telepaths? Had she sensed him before?

It was a bit of a leap, but it was all she had. Frey took a deep breath and centered her thoughts while allowing her telepathic senses to roam outward.

There.

Anger, rage, *fear...*

Frey opened her eyes. If she could find him before the rest of the crew were alerted to his presence, she might be able to prevent further bloodshed. Focusing on her slight sense of him, she left her lab, took a sharp right turn and headed back to the kitchens.

EINARR PAUSED, his breathing ragged, his breath still frosting in the warm air. Nothing made sense. He'd thought he was free, but now he was encased in some kind of metallic humming maze. Had he been swallowed by a great beast? Was Odin demanding one more act of valor before he was allowed into the hallowed halls of Valhalla?

He gripped the shaft of his axe more tightly and heard a scuttling sound to his left. Reaching out, he gently pushed open the nearest door and found himself in a space that smelled of food. His stomach grumbled loudly in the silence, convincing him that he was indeed alive and not completely immersed in the nightmare of his dreams. Two green orbs flashed at his shoulder level and he went to grab the creature, whatever it was, and encountered sharp claws and the hiss of fangs.

"Kottur."

He hastily withdrew his hand and sucked his fingers into his mouth. His blood flowed as sluggishly as a frozen river. Cats were beloved of Freyja. Perhaps this was a sign that he was not alone in this strange world? The sound of the cat jumping down to the floor and rubbing against his ankles was surprisingly comforting. When was the last time he'd been touched by another creature?

Moving further into the chamber that smelled like food, he found another door and went inside. Even in the darkness, he could make out the sight of the loaded shelves. The cat had followed him, and was now meowing, but Einarr's focus was on feeding himself. He picked things up at random and discarded them, his mouth watering as his sense of smell returned. Eventually, he found something he recognized and fought with the strange wrapping, using his teeth to rip off the strange coating so that he could bite into the bread beneath.

Carrying the loaf in his hand he searched for a jug or a barrel of ale but found nothing. Frustrated now, he left the food store and returned to the outer room, his keen hearing honing in on the drip of water onto a metal surface. Moving quietly around the space, he found the water and patiently cupped his hands beneath the trickle of liquid until he had satisfied his thirst.

It probably wasn't wise to eat or drink anything in this strange place, but he was too hungry to care if the spirits intended to lure him into another world. He was beginning to believe he was in a cursed realm anyway. Since stepping over the body of the man who'd been caught up in his violent release from the ice, he'd seen no one but the cat. Yet he sensed someone, had recognized the female's thoughts from the moment he'd regained that first sense of himself within the ice.

Someone touched his mind, and he immediately went for his weapon and then paused. Didn't he want to be found? Didn't he yearn for someone to confront him and tell him what was going on? And if it was the female whose presence had reached him even through the ice and his magical entrapment, he might even welcome her...

There was another door that led into what looked like a hall with benches and tables set out for eating. But as he came through it, that wasn't what caught his attention. Set in the wall was two large clear rectangles that looked out into...*nothingness.* His newly beating heart almost stopped as he tried to comprehend what he was seeing. Somehow he was flying through the night sky and the stars. But he didn't recognize any of the constellations.

Closing his eyes, he sank to his knees and prayed desperately to his Gods.

FREY PAUSED at the junction of the two passages and listened carefully. Something was moving around in the kitchen attached to the mess hall. Gripping her weapon tightly, she advanced toward the half-open door and peered into the darkness. A faucet dripped and somewhere Armstrong, the ship's cat was purring.

Armstrong only purred when he was fed or he had company. There was another door that led out of the small galley kitchen back into the mess hall. It was possible that her Viking was either hiding in the galley, or had moved through into the next room.

She relaxed her psychic shields a little more and stifled a gasp. He was close, his thoughts a strange mixture of overwhelming fear and murderous intent. It made her want to find him and help him through this terrifying transition into a new and unfathomable world--if he didn't kill her at first sight. In preparation for the trip she'd read a lot about the Vikings and their reputation as fearless warriors and ruthless enemies.

And he wouldn't be happy right now.

She forced herself to keep moving and entered the kitchen, inhaling its usual uneasy blend of cooking oil and harsh cleaning fluids. The door to the food storage unit was open and Frey hesitated outside it. The Viking wasn't there. Considering the mess he'd left behind, he'd obviously been foraging for food. She could only imagine what he'd made of space rations.

She went onward, ignoring the cat, and headed back into the mess hall. The door was ajar. She crouched down to look through the small gap and immediately saw the silhouette of a man kneeling on the floor. The ground level security lighting was minimal, but she knew she wasn't looking at a member of the crew. This man was too large and too *different*.

"*Komdu hingað.*"

She stiffened as a brusque command infiltrated her mind. The language was unknown, the compulsion to stand up and meet her fate was almost impossible to resist.

Readjusting her grip on her weapon, she pocketed it and drew out her FREN authorized stun gun, making sure it was loaded and ready to rock. Getting to her feet, she pushed the door fully open and took one unsteady step forward.

The Viking turned his head toward her, and she caught a glimpse of sharp white teeth and a ferocious scowl. As he rose to a crouch, she pointed the stun gun at him and aimed at the place where his neck met his shoulder. The next few seconds were a blur as he lunged for her, knocking the gun from her hand. His fingers wrapped around her throat and she had no choice but to look at him.

"hver ert þú?"

Frey tried to swallow. "I can't understand you."

He repeated the question, his mind echoing the same words.

"I don't know, what you are saying, let me help you, I can..."

"Frey? What's going on?" Slavin's voice cut across the Viking's unintelligible answer.

"Can't..." Frey was wheezing for breath now, unable to get through to the man squeezing the life out of her.

Security alarms blared, and with a snarl, the Viking dropped her to the floor and ran toward the door. The sound of running feet and a sudden yell reverberated down the hallway, and then Brown was by her side, his expression furious.

"Are you all right?" He hauled her onto a chair and held her steady as she gasped for breath. "What the hell happened, Tecky? Why didn't you sound the alarm sooner?"

"Was trying to find the Viking, to see if he had really survived." She coughed. "Was going to call for back up as soon as I'd verified that."

She leaned back against the table as the mess hall filled with crew members in various states of undress and aggravation. Slavin arrived and came over to Frey.

"Are you okay? I thought you were going to die."

Frey managed a shaky grin. "I'm fine, honestly."

"Heeze...don't ever do that to me again. I thought—"

Frey cut across her friend. *"Can you sense the Viking? Telepathically I mean?"*

"I'm not sure." Slavin frowned. *"There's something there, but it's very faint. Why, can you?"*

"What the hell is going on here?"

Frey jumped as Captain Travis strode into the room.

"Turn off the alarms," he barked at Brown. "What's the situation, Tecky?"

Frey stood up, aware of Slavin at her shoulder, and faced the irate captain. "The Viking appears to be alive and somewhere on the ship, sir."

Travis opened his mouth and then shut it again. *"What?"*

"I don't know what happened, sir. I woke up early and decided to go down to the lab where I found Security Officer Prism dead and all three of the security doors blown apart."

"So you're suggesting our frozen cargo somehow managed to get himself out of a block of ice, kill one of my team and escape into the ship without anyone apart from you being fucking aware of it?" He glared at her. "Why didn't you fucking sound the alarms the instant you realized Prism was dead? Why didn't the alarms sound in the first place?"

Slavin cleared her throat. "FREN took responsibility for security in the lab. It's highly probable that they disconnected the area from the main sensors."

"Which still doesn't explain why Tecky here didn't raise the alarm herself."

Frey met his enraged gaze. "Because I thought it was my responsibility to locate the Viking before I called in security."

"And what the hell made you think that?"

Frey raised her chin. "My orders from FREN were to take control of the situation and direct others on the ship as I saw fit."

"FREN told you that?"

"Yes, sir."

"Fuck them. I'm captain of this ship until I'm told otherwise and you, Science Officer Frey, are suspended from duty while I find and catch this Viking and put him in a holding cell."

"Sir, I have to warn you that he is bound to be confused about where he is. He doesn't even speak our language."

"I'm sure he'll understand a gun pointed at his head."

"No, sir he *won't*. He's never seen a gun before in his life." Frey swallowed with some difficulty. It wasn't in her nature to stand up to anyone in authority or create problems. "FREN have authorized me to deal with him. I would appreciate it if you let me carry out my orders. I—"

He cut her off with a decisive wave of his hand. "I'm the captain of this ship. You are confined to quarters. When I have the Viking in a controlled and secure environment, I will allow you to check him over and pass the information on to FREN."

"But—" Frey took an impulsive step forward. Brown's hand closed around her elbow and proved impossible to shake off. "Please, don't kill him, Captain. *Please* let me deal with him. I have the necessary tools to sedate the male and to help him understand what we are saying to him."

"Your observations and objections have been noted." Captain Travis paused in the doorway to look back at her. "As I said, you can check him out when I've found him and prevented him from damaging my ship or killing any more of my crew."

The remaining two security members followed the captain out, leaving Brown waiting patiently at Frey's side. Frey turned to him.

"Please make sure Captain Travis checks his messages this morning. I'm fairly certain he will have heard from both FREN and the TSA about this situation and how I'm expected to deal with it."

Brown lowered his voice "He's already checked his messages. That's why he was delayed. He just doesn't choose to acknowledge the orders."

"But that's…"

He gripped her elbow tighter. "Come on, Tecky. Let's get you to medical to check out your throat and then back to your quarters."

As she was marched along to the medical center, Frey's mind was in turmoil. If Travis cornered the Viking and killed him, her career would be over and FREN would probably make sure no one on the ship ever went into space again in any capacity. And the Viking would be dead, and that was unacceptable.

"What can I do to help, Frey?"

Frey hesitated at Slavin's gentle question. *"Nothing unless you're prepared to go against captain's orders. I need to get to the Viking before Travis corners him. I have a feeling he won't give up very easily."*

"Who, Travis or the Viking?" Slavin asked.

"The four-thousand-year-old warrior. The one with the axe and probably a few daggers hidden around his person. Vikings believed that the best death imaginable was in battle."

"Damn." Slavin paused. *"He didn't kill you though, did he?"*

"No, he just punched the tranq gun out of my hand and tried to choke me."

She didn't tell Slavin that the Viking had attempted to communicate telepathically with her. That was still too complicated to think about, let alone share. For some reason, they were linked and now she'd been denied any opportunity to find and secure him.

Brown opened the door into medical and guided Frey through it. A body lay on one of the gurneys with a sheet drawn up over it. She guessed it was the unfortunate Prism who'd either been caught in the explosion or killed by the emerging Viking. Rehm, one of the pilots from the bridge was also there holding a cloth to a deep slashing cut on the side of his head. He must have been the guy she'd heard scream after the Viking dropped her to the floor.

The medic looked up as he tended to Rehm and gestured to a chair.

"Take a seat, Tecky. I have to seal this wound up."

Frey sat and concentrated her attention on anything *but* the smell of blood, and the unmoving mound on the gurney.

SOMEONE WAS COMING and it wasn't the cat, or his female…

Einarr crouched between the two towering metal structures and focused his gaze on the outline of the door several lengths away from him. He wasn't sure where he was, but the cylinders gave him good cover and the ability to ambush his adversaries if it became necessary.

But what if he killed them all? From what he'd already seen, these men didn't carry any weapons. Were they like the Christian monks his ancestors had plundered and robbed when the Vikings first discovered the riches of England? A defenseless peaceful people who had no ability to fight back?

But the female had pointed some kind of weapon at him, he was quite certain of that. He had no idea how many people inhabited this strange place that seemed to float through the night skies like a giant bird or a sea-less wind-less ship.

He hunkered down as the voices grew louder. She'd been a little thing with hair the color of an autumn leaf and wide startled brown eyes. But she hadn't understood him at all, even in her thoughts, which worried him immensely. If these people were peaceful and were simply a means to get him to Valhalla or wherever the Gods wanted him to be, he needed to speak to them. He wasn't like his ancestors. He'd learned to parley with those who deserved it.

And in this instance, he was the one who needed to understand where he was and exactly what was going on. He considered putting away his axe and stepping out with his hands raised, but he couldn't do that either. He might not be as rabid as his ancestors, but he was no coward, and until he gauged the intent of the men coming after him, he would be a fool to relax his guard.

He squinted through the darkness. There were three of them in a single line, one carried an extremely bright source of light that he directed into every shadowed area. The others carried something in their hands, which he had to assume were weapons of unknown strength. He slid his axe back into his belt and selected a throwing dagger instead.

As he pondered his choices, he felt an all-too familiar tingle in his fingers and the runes on his armbands began to glow. Einarr smiled into the darkness. His magic was returning. Unfortunately for his opponents, he had another source of power beyond that of his strength. He had the magic of a hundred seers in his blood—right back to his ancestor Odin. If strength would not or could not defeat a man's enemies, there was always another way. In truth, unlike his brother Aki, he'd always used violence as a last resort.

Eventually, the powerful light swung toward his hiding place. Lifting his hand, palm facing outward, he reflected the beam back toward his pursuers, getting his first good look at the two brawny males and the man behind them who was obviously in charge. Even as they complained about the sudden unexpected reflection, he magicked a cloud around himself, distorting his image and making him disappear into the shadows. If they were like most men, they wouldn't be able to see him at all.

With a sign from their commander, they moved on deeper into the space leaving Einarr in peace. He was just about to relax when one of the men turned back, his expression puzzled, and came straight toward Einarr's hiding place. With a silent curse, Einarr caught the man around the neck and silenced him dropping the unconscious body to the floor and taking the "weapon" for further examination.

He knew he'd have to move again. Following his instincts, he searched out a series of ladders that took him even further into the bowels of the ship and set about finding a secure place to get some rest.

4

FREY SAT UP STRAIGHT AS A SECURITY GUARD WAS BROUGHT INTO the already cramped medical facility and placed on the last remaining gurney. The doc turned away from examining her throat and grimaced.

"Another one? What's going on?"

"We have a defrosted Viking running around the ship. What else do you need to know?" Brown snapped. "What happened, Ross?"

"We're not sure." The man who'd brought the new patient in paused at the door. "We made a sweep of storage bay one. The captain and I were at the door ready to move out when we realized Moshe wasn't with us. I retraced our path and found him like this." Ross shook his head. "I have to get back. The captain's waiting for me."

The doctor looked up from his examination. "Tell the captain Moshe's been knocked unconscious with a blow to the side of the head. He'll have a slight concussion, but otherwise he'll be fine. In fact, he's coming around now."

As Ross left, Brown moved over to stand by the gurney. "Moshe? What happened?"

His much younger colleague groaned as the doctor gave him a shot in the arm. "Jeez, that scared the fuck out of me."

"What did?" Brown asked with an edge to his voice.

"We scanned the storage bay, checked it out and found nothing, and then I got this sense, this kind of *tickling* sensation in the back of my neck, you know? So I had to turn around and go back. And *shit*, this huge dude was just suddenly there and that was the last thing I remember."

"Where's your weapon?"

Moshe sighed. "Shit, *I* don't know. I certainly didn't get to use it. He was too damned fast."

"Nice attitude for a security operative, Moshe," Brown muttered.

"You wouldn't have done any better. One moment there was nothing except this grey fog and then suddenly that guy was *right in my face*." He shuddered. "Did I mention that he was fucking *huge*?"

"So he's a *magical* Viking, is he?"

"Maybe. He certainly knows how to hide his tracks."

Despite Brown's sarcastic tone, Frey considered Ross's words very carefully. The Viking was telepathic and his ability to survive in ice for thousands of years hinted at other powers… As a Pavlovan, she knew her Gods were magical and often did extraordinary things. She'd also noticed that those from Earth didn't seem to have much faith in anything at all.

Both Captain Travis and Brown were from Earth. Moshe was half-Pavlovan which might explain why he'd had to go and check out that feeling.

"If the Viking has acquired one of our weapons, Brown, it might cause a problem if he inadvertently sets it off." Frey said as calmly as she could. "Perhaps you should inform the captain."

"I'll do that as soon as I've returned you to your quarters."

Frey slid off the gurney and re-buttoned her uniform. "You

should just let *me* tell him and how I intend to deal with the problem."

"Nice try, Tecky, but you're not going near the captain, or that Viking until I'm given the okay."

Freya held his gaze. "Then you won't catch him, and more of our crew will be injured. Is that what you want?"

"And you think you can save the day?"

"Yes."

His smile was somewhere between kind and dismissive. "Let's get you safely back to your quarters, shall we?"

Frey let out her breath and stomped down the path to the crew quarters, glad that she had her own cabin to fret and fume in alone. Brown opened the door and ushered her inside.

"Have a good evening, Tecky."

She let him do his thing, heard him tapping away at the security panel changing the access codes so that she couldn't leave without setting off an alert. He had no idea that as a Pavlovan, she had the telepathic ability to manipulate electrical signals, get out of that door in less than a second, and reset the alarms to make it look as if she'd never left.

But first, she needed to check her emergency supplies from FREN, form a plan and make sure she knew where her Viking was hiding. This time she would come prepared for a fight.

IT WAS warm down in the innards of whatever magical flying boat Einarr was currently on. He'd finished the loaf of excellent bread and drank most of the water he'd decanted into his leather-drinking pouch. Now he was waiting for either another attack or the reappearance of his female. He had no doubt that she would find him. He believed in the Fates and she, whoever she was, had become part of his destiny, he could sense it.

Time passed slowly, the warmth of his hiding place and the

regular roar of whatever powered the ship making him yawn and fight sleep. He didn't want to sleep. Some part of him feared that if he did so, he'd wake up in another world and he would finally go mad.

He jerked awake and inhaled sharply as the scent of his female's blood reached him and allowed his mind to relax its vigil. Her thoughts briefly touched his in a moment of recognition as intimate as the brushing of their lips together. He stayed where he was, his axe in plain view on the floor by his side, his throwing dagger in his left hand. Her silhouette grew closer until she blocked out all the light behind her.

She went down on all fours and crawled very slowly toward him and then sat back on her heels. Even in the darkness he drank in her sweetness, the full curve of her lower lip and the fullness of her breasts.

"komdu hérna."

He sent the thought to her and held out his hand, willing her to understand him and come to him. When she moved forward and grasped his fingers it was as if a thunderbolt shuddered through him and his cock hardened in a sudden aching rush. He growled and tightened his grip in case she had any thoughts of changing her mind and retreating.

He urged her closer until she was practically in his lap, which suited him perfectly, because once she opened her legs he could be inside her in seconds. She tugged on his hand and he reluctantly released her only to shiver as she placed her fingers on his cheek and stared right into his eyes. He let the dagger fall gently to the floor aware only of her soft breathing and the pounding of his heart.

"Blóð af blóði mínu."

He licked a line along the seam of her lips and she moaned something. Cupping her head in his hands he gently kissed her until she was kissing him back, her tongue in his mouth, her teeth nipping at his lips and…

"Fjandi!" He tried to jerk his head away but it was too late. The she-devil pierced his skin with something and everything went black...

FREY LET OUT her breath in a sudden rush as the Viking beneath her went still. She could only hope that the stun gun would hold him long enough to secure him in a safe place. Gods, he'd tasted so fine she hadn't wanted to stop kissing him. She made sure he was still breathing and then focused on the task at hand.

"Slavin? Get Brown and his team down to the engine room ASAP. I have the Viking."

EINARR WAS aware of being lifted and carried out of his hiding place, his female walked in front of him holding open the doors. She'd betrayed him. Anger coalesced in his gut and the metal of his armbands grew warm illuminating the runes etched into their surfaces in the darkness.

As if she sensed the emergence of his magic, the female raised some kind of alarm and pointed at him. It was too late. He was already on the move, smashing his fist into one of the men who carried him whilst sending a burst of magical power through the second. As both men went down, Einarr rolled over and came back to his feet, his hand already shooting out to grab the female.

She screamed once as he slammed his hand over her mouth and drew her hard against his chest, his dagger at her throat. The other male took one look at him and backed away, his mouth moving, his words unintelligible as he spoke urgently to the captive female.

Without waiting, Einarr pivoted on his heel and began to

drag his female back to where he'd made his stand before. She tried to fight him, but he was twice her size and still enraged by her dishonorable tactics. She struggled to free one hand and slapped it against his neck.

With a growl, he caught her fingers and threw her over his shoulder. Her breath slammed out as he picked up the pace and jogged down the tight passageway between the tall iron containers. Eventually, he let her down, but wrapped a hand around her throat to keep her exactly where he could see her. He used his other hand to investigate his neck.

"Don't take that off."

His fingers froze.

"It's a universal translator strip, FREN programmed it with Old Norse."

He felt the edges of something foreign against his skin but didn't remove it. She twisted around to gaze up at him, her brown eyes wide.

"You can understand me now, right?"

He nodded.

"Great." She swallowed hard, her throat working against the blade of his dagger. "So, could you put the knife away while we talk?"

He shook his head and her skin went pale.

"You can't understand me?"

He sank down to his knees bringing her with him, her back to his chest, one of his hands still at her throat, the other around her hips. On impulse he leaned forward and buried his face in her hair inhaling her flowery scent and the throb of her blood beneath her skin. With great care he bit down on the curve of her throat until she jumped.

"My female," he growled.

"I certainly am not yours,"

"Mine." He bit harder, and she tried to pull out of his grasp. "Mine by blood and magic."

"I'm not magic and my blood is my own, thank you very much."

"You will change your mind when you are under me begging for my cock and my seed."

"I…will not! That's disgusting, I—"

He wrapped her ponytail around his fingers and drew her face to his for a savage kiss. "You will beg."

She bit his lip and he cursed and released his grip on her hair.

Her bravery impressed him. He settled her closer within the grip of his thighs until her arse was against his leather-clad groin. His cock kicked up and he fought a groan. He'd have her soon; have her spread beneath him while he fucked her hard but not yet, not quite yet.

"They'll be coming to get you," she whispered. "There isn't anywhere for you to run."

"I don't run."

The last time he'd done that, he'd been encased in ice by a fickle and demanding God.

"Good," she breathed. "Then put down your weapons, and we can work this out."

"Nay." He pressed the edge of his dagger against her throat. "Tell me, sorceress how you called me from my sleep."

"I didn't do anything,"

"You lie."

She shivered. "There was an eclipse. The systems went haywire. You just appeared out of nowhere."

"I do not understand your words." He pressed a little harder. "Your blood called me. I felt it in my soul."

"That makes no sense. I didn't call you I—" She went still and then started talking, babbling like a brook in high season making it difficult for him to follow her. "I pricked my finger, there was one drop of blood, but it came from the ice, it wasn't… oh dear Gods, what happened?"

"You *called* to me."

She subsided against him. "Well something happened because here you are. Maybe it was both, the eclipse *and* the blood."

"What is this eclipse?"

"When the planets aligned and covered the Pavlovan moons of Odin and Thor."

He didn't understand half her words, but at least something made sense. "You know of my Gods?"

"I've studied up on them." She sighed. "Will you *please* put the dagger away? You're scaring me."

He looked down at her auburn head. "Nay."

"I won't let them hurt you."

"Let them?" He snorted. "I am a match for any man. I do not hide behind my womenfolk."

"You can't win this one. You have no idea where you are, what's been happening, or where you are going."

"This could be one of Floki's tricks. I could be dreaming the whole thing."

"I wish I was dreaming." She tried to straighten and then winced as his blade grazed her neck. "I can't let you run around this ship killing people and destroying things."

"That decision isn't yours to make, woman."

"You're kidding, right? I can give the order to have you shot right now."

"And kill yourself?"

"We have weapons that could take you out and not damage a hair on my head. Please believe me."

He picked up the stick he'd taken from the guard and tossed it in his palm. "This *paltry* thing?"

Her fingers closed around his wrist. "For the Gods sake, put it *down*! If it goes off, it could take out the engines of this ship or rip through the hull, and we'd all plummet to our deaths."

He considered that, his fingers moving over the shining

metal tube and handle. "But I wish to die gloriously in battle and take my place in Valhalla."

"Oh *please*, don't say that." She hesitated. "Don't you wish to see if your companion survived the ice, too?"

He stiffened. "My brother Aki is here?"

"Not on this ship. He is being taken to Alpha Three to be defrosted just like you were."

"De-frosted?"

"You were both found encased in ice in the city of York on Earth. Alpha Base Three is the only place in this planetary alliance with the necessary technology to even attempt to bring you back to life."

Again, almost nothing she said made sense. "But I am alive." He flexed his muscles.

"That wasn't supposed to happen yet."

"Then perhaps my brother is alive, too."

She tried to turn her head to look at him. "I could find out, but you'd have to let me go."

"Or I can accompany you while you find out."

She dug her elbow into his side. "You're not being very cooperative."

"Why should I be? You've already deceived me once."

"Because it's safer for you to be in a controlled environment where we can talk without anyone getting hurt."

Einarr snorted. "As if such a place exists. No man can be trusted."

"Not even your brother?"

FREY GASPED as the Viking lifted her up and turned her to face him. It was the first time she'd gotten a good look at his eyes, which were the pale blue of a husky dog and far icier. His black hair was shaved on the sides, braided at the back and then gathered at the base of his neck. It wasn't a handsome face, but it was a compelling one. She knew she'd never forget him. But how to persuade him to come out of hiding and release her?

He shrugged as though he didn't have a care in the world. "My brother can take care of himself."

"Alone?" She blinked slowly at him. "Don't you want to see him again?"

A muscle flexed in his square jaw, and Frey resisted an urge to touch his unsmiling mouth. He'd sat her across his lap, her thighs spread over his crossed knees her sex pressed against his groin. She could feel the throbbing heat of his concealed cock inches from the sudden wet need of her arousal. The reality of his presence was a million times better than the fevered dreams she'd had since embarking on the voyage. She'd dreamed of being his, of being tangled up naked in bed with him while they fucked for hours... And she was aroused now. She wanted to strip him out of his leathers and lick his skin...

His blue eyes narrowed, and he spread his fingers over her ass, pushing her even closer to the stiff temptation of his erection. She brought her hand up and braced it against his massive chest.

"Let me go."

"You want me," he said quietly.

"I don't know what you are talking about."

"I think you understand me very well." He rocked his hips. "I can smell your desire, and you know I am already hard for you."

She felt her cheeks heat. "It's not that simple."

"Aye it is. I free my cock and I'll be inside you in less than a moment." He glanced down at his lap. "I'm big. I would satisfy you well."

She smothered a groan as he settled her even more intimately over him. "It wouldn't be a good idea."

"Why not?"

"Because..." She glared at him. "Because it wouldn't, okay?

Just because I'm acting a little weirdly around a telepath doesn't mean there's anything in particular going on, like I want to mate with you or anything..." Frey stopped speaking. Oh dear Gods. This was exactly like the health unit Teacher Forbes had shown them during their junior space camp training: *The inconvenient nature of telepathic attraction and finding mates where you least expect them.* But this male was a four-thousand-year-old Viking! He wasn't Pavlovan or even an Etruscan.

He was her science project.

And she wanted to fuck him more than she wanted to breathe.

"What is wrong?"

His low voice made her jump.

"Nothing! As I said, we need to get you into a safe and secure area." She was aware that she was jabbering and that he still held her tightly against the big, hard, hot rod of his cock...

"You want me." He slowly inhaled. "I need to fuck you. I can sense your desire in your blood."

"Which doesn't mean anything," she snapped back. "Now behave yourself and come and be officially welcomed by the captain and crew."

He cupped her cheek, his remarkable eyes moving over her face. "Nay."

She moaned as he bent his head and took her mouth in a savage kiss of possession. His hands shifted, locking her hard against his body until she was rubbing herself shamelessly against him like Armstrong the cat. Her clit was throbbing, her nipples were hard, and she was so wet that if he'd touched her sex she'd easily take his cock.

"Not easily. I'm big. I'd need to get you ready with my mouth and my fingers." he crooned to her as his mouth ravished hers. *"But by Odin, I would serve you well."*

She thought she whimpered. She couldn't even protect her most intimate thoughts from him. Kissing him was more arousing than having full sex with any of her previous partners. It just felt so right. As if she'd been waiting for this moment for the whole of her life. It was *incredible.* Oh Gods, if she kept this up she was going to come and he was bound to notice, and then he'd fuck her, and she wouldn't be able to stop him, maybe for days, and...

"*Just hold him there.*"

Even as she recognized Slavin's voice the big Viking beneath her jerked and went still, his head falling back to strike against the metal storage unit behind him. A dart bristled in the crease of his neck.

No! Had she screamed that out loud? She hoped she hadn't. Frey forced herself to slide out of the Viking's arms and step away. Brown and his two assistants picked the unconscious form up and this time took off as fast as they could to the tiny brig.

"Are you okay?" Slavin crouched down beside her.

"Not really." Frey forced down a shudder of pure, frustrated lust.

Slavin grinned. "You looked like you were quite enjoying being mauled."

"I was." Frey stood up. "He's a telepath"

"I got that. He isn't very clear to me."

"He's *way* too clear to me." She switched into telepathic mode. "*I'm struggling to keep my hands off him.*"

Slavin put her hand on Frey's arm. "*What?*"

"*Yeah, I'm not sure what's going on.*"

"*Well, they do say we might meet our mates anywhere.*" Slavin gave her a tentative grin. "*My instructor at university was Etruscan and was brought here by a Pavlovan soldier after her unit abandoned her during a mission.*"

"*That's slightly different to a four-thousand year old Viking.*" Frey started walking again. "*I feel like such a fool. How am I going to explain this to my mothers?*"

"You're that certain he's the one?"

"Well, he's one of the one's," Frey muttered. *I feel it in my soul."* She squared her shoulders. It felt stupid even saying such dramatic and life changing words, but she'd learned never to lie to herself. "And now I have to forget all of that and just make sure he stays alive."

5

EINARR CONSIDERED THE SHACKLES THAT HAD BEEN PUT ON HIS ankles and wrists and how easily he could remove them. There was also something attached to his upper arm through a long needle buried in his skin. The healer had told him it was for *nutritional purposes*, whatever that meant. Brown, one of his guards had simplified the matter and said it was food and water and necessary to keep him alive.

He'd developed a grudging respect for Brown who didn't treat him like a fool, but also refused to leave him alone for a second. Not that he couldn't escape in the blink of an eye… His female had made a good point. Learning where he was and about his brother's fate could only help him plan his future escape. He'd already decided that whatever happened he would be taking his woman with him.

Apart from the bars on the door, the cell bore no resemblance to any similar structure he'd been incarcerated in on an unsuccessful raid. There was no wood, only smooth white surfaces that resisted his attempts to break them. He slammed his fist against the unforgiving wall and then continued his pacing. The lights were giving him a headache and were brighter than the noon sun. He hated this place. It made him yearn to fight his way out with whatever weapons he could find and destroy everything.

The door unlocked from the outside and Brown stood to attention as another older man came in. Einarr recognized him as one of the men who'd been hunting him earlier.

"I'm Travis, captain of this vessel."

Einarr inclined his head an inch and kept his gaze bland.

"We wish you no harm, Viking. Our intention is to take you to Alpha Three where you will be reunited with your companion from the ice."

Travis sat down as Einarr continued to study him before taking the seat opposite. Eventually, Travis looked back over his shoulder at the guard and asked.

"Can he understand me, Brown?"

"Yes, sir. The translator is working perfectly."

"Then he's not choosing to cooperate."

"I wouldn't say that either, sir. He's still sitting here."

"You believe he's a security risk?"

"Yes, sir. Despite his advanced age he has unusual abilities."

Reluctant to allow the captain's thoughts to stray in that direction, Einarr sat forward. "I understand. Where is the female?"

"Which one?"

"The one who trapped me."

"You mean Slavin? She shot the tranquilizer dart at you, but it was on my orders."

"Not her. The one who ensnared me with her kisses."

An expression of discomfort crossed the captain's face. "Science Officer Frey is confined to her quarters until we reach Alpha Three."

"I want her."

"She is not available."

"Then we have nothing more to say to each other." Einarr

turned away and lay down on his bunk, his gaze on the shining white ceiling.

"What do you mean?" Travis blustered. "I am authorized to negotiate with you."

Einarr didn't bother to reply. Either they wanted to talk to him and they fetched his female, or he'd go and find her himself.

After another muttered conversation, the captain left. Brown sighed and sat down again.

"You've done it now, mate. The captain doesn't take kindly to anyone undermining his authority, and he's already got it in for our Science Officer."

Her name was Frey…like the goddess.

Closing his eyes and radiating a sense of complete relaxation, Einarr sought Frey in his mind. She wasn't in pain, or in fear of her life. That was good. She was, however angry and frustrated. He felt the same. Having her in his arms had felt right somehow—as if she belonged there. He didn't question such feelings. They came from the Gods and the source of his magic. She called to his blood. That was enough.

Smiling, he remembered how her lips felt and the way she'd stroked and sucked his tongue into her mouth. How would her lips feel parted around his thick rod? How would his mouth feel against the wetness of her lower lips as he plunged his tongue inside her?

His cock stirred and he cupped a hand over it.

"*Stop it, Viking.*" Frey's voice echoed in his head.

He ran a finger along the hardness of his shaft as she responded to him. The thought of having her, of finally possessing her flesh, was the only thing that made sense to him in this frightening world. "*I'm thinking how I'm going to make you scream when I put my mouth on your cunt and plunge my tongue deep inside you.*"

"*You're not going to do anything of the kind. You're in the brig.*"

She sounded…disappointed.

"Do not doubt me. Frey, I will have you naked and under me before very long. You'll scream for me. I know it."

"When I'm locked in my cabin?"

"If you want me, I'll come to you."

"Yeah, right."

He wasn't sure what her words meant, but he knew she doubted him. And, in truth, he wasn't sure he could magic himself to her side in this strange cold metal ship, but he would certainly try if she needed him. And if he couldn't get out, perhaps he could make sure she came to him.

He opened one eye and glanced over at Brown. Perhaps it was time to be diplomatic.

"Tell your captain that I am willing to speak to him, but only if the woman Frey is present."

FREY STOOD up as her cabin door was unlocked and she tried to look calm as Ross came in, his weapon out and armed. This whole situation was crazy and not how she had envisioned meeting one of her mates at all. Her birth mother had told her that meeting her First Male had been unforgettable and that even though he'd later deserted their family, she still loved him. Frey hadn't understood or accepted any of that until the thought of *not* seeing the Viking again made her want to scream and pull out her hair. Which was a ridiculous way to feel about someone you had only just met—even if they had shoved their tongue down your throat and made you want to throw off your clothes and simply fuck them forever.

"Tecky? Come on, you're wanted."

She followed him down the passageway, aware of a second armed security guard behind her. They halted at the holding room next to the brig, and Ross held onto her arm.

"Go in slowly and keep your hands visible. The Viking and Captain Travis are already at the table."

Frey did as she was told blinking at the stark lighting of the cell and the minimum furnishings. Her Viking sat on one side of the table, his wrists shackled, his fingers linked together. He looked up as she entered the room, his icy blue gaze fixing on her. She couldn't look away. After a long moment, he stared down at the scarred white table top, and she was able to breathe again.

"Tecky." Captain Travis gestured for her to sit beside him. "I've already told our guest that I am willing to answer any questions he has. He insisted that you were present for his debriefing." He fixed her with a compelling stare. "I expect you to follow my lead and only answer when I give you permission to speak. Do you understand?"

"Yes, Captain." Frey took a seat.

Being so close to the Viking meant she could finally study the intricate leatherwork of his jerkin and the tattoos that encircled his wrist and moved up his left arm disappearing within his sleeve. Runes marked the sides of his shaved scalp and his crow-colored hair was woven and plaited together into one single braid. Her fingers curled and uncurled. Did he ever untie his hair? How would it look flowing freely over his shoulders?

"Tecky…"

She jumped and returned her attention to Travis.

"Yes, Sir?"

"Pay attention."

"Yes, Sir." It was proving hard to do that when all she wanted to do was leap over the table and grab any part of the Viking she could get her hands on and lick him…

"I would like it if you did that. You could start with my cock."

His thought floated over to her, and she realized he was staring at her mouth. She licked her lips, and he straightened in his seat. This was ridiculous. Her career was on the line and she was simpering like a teenager at the local bad boy.

"What is your name?" Travis asked.

"Einarr Bloodaxe."

"What is the last thing you remember, Einarr?"

"Before waking up here?"

At Travis's nod, the Viking leaned back in his chair, which creaked ominously.

"I was with my brother. We were attempting to evade our enemies."

"And what happened?"

"I'm not sure." Einarr shrugged, the motion as powerful as a panther's. "One moment we were running, the next...we were caught within the ice."

Frey stared hard at him, aware that although he was telling the truth, he wasn't revealing everything. He didn't look directly at her but she knew he was as aware of her as she was of him. She'd heard stories about how it felt to "meet your mate," but she hadn't imagined it would be so...powerful and primitive. If it were up to her, she'd drag him off to her cabin, get him naked and keep him there forever.

His knee bumped against hers under the table and she jumped. Travis shot an irritated glance at her and she realized he'd been speaking.

"Anything to add, Science Officer?"

"Only that I have informed FREN and Alpha Base Three about your present condition, Einarr, and have asked for information about the other ship. Due to interference from the eclipse and the current positions of the planets Thor and Odin, I haven't received a reply yet."

He nodded. "Thank you."

"You're welcome."

Travis cleared his throat. "Do you wish me to explain where you are now?"

"That would be helpful."

Einarr looked and sounded far more relaxed than he felt. Frey had a sudden image of a caged feline pacing back and forth waiting to strike. Should she warn the captain?

"I won't hurt them unless I have to, Frey."

His thought came through clearly to her. It was disconcerting to have someone reading her mind so easily.

"You are currently on a space ship bound for Alpha Base Three a research lab on one of Odin's moons."

Einarr's smile was dismissive. "I do not understand most of your words. I also do not understand how we appear to be sailing through the night sky. I thought at first that I was dreaming—perhaps I still am."

"You were encased in ice for a very long time." Travis said carefully. "Things have changed. Technology has advanced our understanding of our world and the universe around it."

A slight crease appeared between Einarr's brows. "How long was I asleep for?"

Travis took a deep breath. "About four thousand Earth years."

"Four *thousand*? When most men are dead at five and forty?" Einarr shook his head. "This is *impossible*. It must be the work of the Gods."

"I assure you that it is not only possible, but true. You are living proof of that. When we get to Alpha Three, there will be a team of experts available to help you adjust to your new life. No one expected you to wake up at this point. We still don't understand why you did."

Einarr half-smiled, the shock still reverberating in his eyes. "The Gods called me." He nodded at Frey. "*She* called me with her blood."

Travis shot her a look. "Are you suggesting Science Officer Frey somehow brought you out of the ice?"

"Aye. Otherwise why else would I be here?"

Silence filled the small space as Captain Travis swung his attention back to Frey.

"Would you care to elaborate on this, Tecky?"

She stared into his eyes. "I did nothing that wasn't authorized by FREN, sir. You can ask them to confirm that when we reestablish contact. Our guest is obviously disoriented and seeking solutions within his own understanding of his religion and culture."

"I am not." Einarr interrupted her. "I know what is right."

"Captain…" Frey ignored him and tried to keep talking. "I did nothing wrong."

"Except join your blood to mine when I was still trapped within the ice."

"I did *not*! I—"

Travis held up his hand. "This is not an appropriate time to discuss the reasons why this happened. Our focus now is on getting Einarr safely to Alpha Three without further injury to him or this crew." He turned to the Viking. "You will remain in the brig under the care of our medical team until we dock at Alpha Three."

"I WILL NOT." Einarr said.

Travis who was in the process of getting to his feet stiffened. "Then you want me to get the doc to knock you out for the remainder of this journey? I can do it, you know."

"I *want* to stay with Frey."

"That's not possible."

"Then I will not cooperate with you." Einarr smiled and lifted his manacled hands. There was a flash of bright light and the metal rings flew off and clattered to the floor.

Weapons clicked and locked ready to fire, surrounding him.

"I am certain you do not wish to harm me, Captain. In truth,

I suspect that your overlords wish very much for me to stay alive." He glanced around the tense circle of armed men. "I wish to be given the freedom of the ship and access to Frey's company and quarters. If you agree to this, I swear on my Gods that I will not harm your crew or damage your ship."

Travis didn't lower his weapon. "I cannot give one of my crew into your hands. I will not have my Science Officer held hostage to your demands."

"She will not consider herself my hostage." Einarr ripped the needle out from his arm, stood up and held out his hand. "Tell your captain that you come to me willingly, Frey."

She took a step toward him, her expression troubled. Her slim fingers slid into his, and he squeezed them hard.

She faced the captain, her chin held high. "If it means the rest of the crew are safe, I'm willing to stay with him, sir."

"Are you sure about this?" Travis asked again.

"Yes."

Travis continued to ignore Einarr and spoke directly to the female. "If we receive fresh information or instructions from FREN, you must promise to obey any orders."

"Of course, sir."

"You are responsible for the good behavior of this man."

"I understand."

Travis stared into Einarr's eyes. "And if you hurt her, you're dead regardless of what Alpha Three or FREN think. You got that?"

"Yes, Captain. You have my word." Einarr studied the other man for a long moment. "On my honor, after sleeping for four thousand years, I do not wish to die *just* yet."

"Good." Travis nodded brusquely. "Keep it that way."

Einarr remained on his feet his hand, gripping Frey's until the shackles were removed from his ankles and the room emptied. His own weapons had been taken from him earlier. He felt naked without his axe and dagger.

"Answer me, Frey." Einarr asked. "How is it that your blood called to mine, and yet you deny it?"

She sat down at the table and he followed her, still grasping her wrist. She heaved a sigh and lowered her gaze.

"I suppose it depends on how you look at it."

"What exactly does that mean?" Einarr frowned at her even though she was avoiding looking at him.

"I was given new codes to input in the probes FREN inserted in the ice. Somehow, I picked up a droplet of ice that looked like a ruby. I *thought* it might be rust or frozen blood from where the probe had touched your scalp, but I had no idea how it got out. I balanced it on my finger and it seemed somehow to prick my skin and I began to bleed." She finally looked up at him her brown gaze worried. "I put my finger in my mouth to suck off the blood. That's all I did, I swear it."

"My blood to your blood. It was enough." Einarr said firmly.

"But it doesn't make sense."

"It does to me."

"How? How the *heeze* can *that* wake you from a four-thousand year sleep?"

He smiled down at her. "Because you are my female, and obviously it was Fated."

"That we'd be on the same ship during an eclipse with planets named Thor and Odin and that one drop of our blood would mix?" She frowned at him. "You do know that is ludicrous, right? And, that the odds of it happening are too small to even calculate. Not that you could even calculate this…"

She drew a shaky breath. Before she could continue, Einarr put his finger over her lips. He'd noticed that she tended to talk a lot when she was nervous. The fact that he made her nervous amused him greatly considering he was the one facing an existence that made no sense.

"It happened, Frey. I am here. You cannot doubt my presence."

She nodded as he brushed his finger over her full lower lip and her mouth opened slightly He wanted to ease his finger between her lips and have her suck on it until he could persuade her to take his cock there instead.

Heat shot through him as she sighed a curse and leaned into him. "This is ridiculous, you know."

"What is?"

"This whole situation."

He pushed his chair back and stood up. "You don't wish to help me?"

"I wish…" Her gaze devoured him making his cock harden in a sudden aching rush. She straightened her shoulders. "I'll show you around the ship, okay?"

"I am at your disposal." He bowed.

His woman was amusing. They both knew she would allow him; nay welcome him, into her bed, yet she held him at bay. She couldn't fool him. The very air throbbed with the force of what was between them He only felt this way when he used his magic during a secret ritual or was in the presence of the Gods.

She'd called him back to life. He had yet to understand the Gods purpose in using her to do so, but he was more than willing to go along with their plans. He was also anxious to hear of Aki's fate. Receiving that information rested on his ability to behave himself. He'd learned early in life that he could only control his own fate and that worrying about others did nothing useful. In his present circumstances, such hard earned patience was very necessary.

Any other man from his village finding himself suddenly aged four thousand years and traveling through the stars would probably have gone mad and hacked his way out of the place. It was only his belief in his Gods and his knowledge of the magical arts that kept him on an even keel. He could only hope that if Aki was awake, he had reacted in the same way.

But would Aki awaken without the lure of a female's blood?

Despite being twins, Aki's temper was far worse than Einarr's. He hoped with all his heart that his brother remained frozen.

Opening the now unlocked door, Frey stepped out into the passageway, nodding at Brown who had stationed himself outside. Einarr paused to appreciate the rear view of his woman in the strange blue garb that covered her like a second skin and displayed the length of her legs and nicely rounded arse. Her red hair was tied back at the neck, displaying the soft skin of her throat. He yearned to set his teeth in that soft hollow and hold onto her while he fucked her from behind…

Her skin flushed pink, and he fought a smile. Soon he would be inside her. He couldn't wait… It was strange. Other things in his world might have changed beyond recognition, but the mating of a man and woman, the *need* to be fucked and touched, remained the same.

He followed her along to the place where he'd found food the previous night. Four new faces gawked at him as Frey introduced him and then offered him something to eat before they moved on.

One of the men came forward and gazed appreciatively up at Einarr.

"You're a big guy. You ate all my bread, didn't you?"

"Aye, it was very good."

The man grinned. "Thanks, I made more. Would you like a sandwich?"

Einarr glanced at Frey who nodded. "You'd probably like it. Do you have any meat to put in the middle, Heald?"

"I have sliced pigcow."

"Then we'll take two of those." Frey touched Einarr's arm. "Come and sit down while Heald makes the sandwiches."

He followed her to one of the tables set close to the clear rectangles showing the stars. While she took a seat, he walked over and placed his palm on the transparent surface. The distortion told him whatever the substance was, it was thick. Did it keep out the blackness much as a strongly made longboat kept out water? A wash of longing for the sea and the simple comforts of home came over him and he briefly closed his eyes.

"Are you okay, Einarr?"

"What is this?" Einarr shook off his melancholy.

"It's like glass." Frey came to stand next to him, her shoulder aligned with his. "You had glass, right?"

"Nothing like this." He smoothed his hand over the surface, "What would happen if it cracked and let in the stars?"

"We'd all die. The ship has to be sealed tight because there isn't any air in space."

"We'd suffocate?"

"Yes, within seconds."

He swiftly took his hand away. With his magical powers, he didn't want to inadvertently kill everyone. The fragrant smell of roasting meat caught his attention and he turned back to the table where Heald was putting out two platters. Each contained a large round of bread with something on top of it and another round of bread atop that.

He sat down on the bench and watched as Frey did the same. She picked up the food and bit into both slabs of bread. He copied her actions and had his portion finished in four bites. The meat smelled better than it tasted.

"What animal is this?" he asked.

Frey, who was only halfway through her first wedge of bread, chewed briskly and wiped her mouth. "It's a genetically constructed creature, which contains elements of both pork and beef. We call it pigcow."

"It tastes unlike anything I have ever had before."

She shrugged. "It's pretty terrible. It's great for space travel because it keeps for years."

"Like dried meat."

"Yes," she looked down at her platter. "Would you like to have the rest of mine? I'm not that hungry."

He frowned at her. "You are already too slender. Finish your food, woman."

"Slender?" She glanced down at her ample bosom. "I think I like you."

After she'd finished, and he'd been given some water and a bright red apple that looked too perfect to eat, they moved on. Einarr kept his attention on the ship and tried to ignore both the huge blackness outside and his fears of what would happen to him next. Nothing about the vessel made sense to him, and the idea that he couldn't simply jump off the side and live was difficult to comprehend.

He tried to remind himself that the Gods had brought him back to life at this point in time for a reason. He might not yet understand their plans, who could? Eventually all would be revealed, and he would collect his reward in Valhalla. He paused to consider the endless darkness outside.

If Valhalla still existed four thousand years in the future... Did anyone worship his Gods anymore? And if they weren't worshipped, had they ceased to exist? Terror stirred in his gut sending cold black fingers of doubt and fear into his mind like a rapidly growing weed.

Frey's voice came back to him, jarring him from his thoughts.

"Am I making sense so far?" She looked back over her shoulder her smile dying. "I know this must be very difficult for you. Tell me to stop when I babble." She pushed a stray lock of hair behind her ear. "I do tend to go on a bit."

"I understand that I am on a vessel in space and that eventually we will land somewhere. That is enough for me." Einarr forced the words out.

Her shoulders sagged. "And I've been rattling on about all kinds of stuff you don't need to know."

He reached out and took her hand, felt her immediate reaction to him. "I enjoy hearing you speak."

"Is there anything you'd like to ask me?" She looked up into his eyes.

"You already know what I want, Frey." He sucked one of her fingers into his mouth. *"You naked, your legs wrapped around my waist, and your fingers clawing my back while I fuck you."*

She swallowed and bit her lip. "I meant anything else about the ship. We still haven't seen my lab or the bridge."

He kissed her hand and then licked her palm. "Then lead on."

The bridge interested him because he could see how it was like navigating a ship at sea. Some of the words the crew used were even familiar to him. There was no chance of him taking control of the ship without him holding a weapon to the captain's head and making him do all the work. He suspected he knew what Captain Travis would say to that idea.

The blond female who had shot him tapped her fingers on some instrument in front of her and watched figures moving on a square shape.

"Everything okay, Frey?" She smiled at Einarr. "Sorry I had to dart you."

He inclined his head. "You must obey orders. I understand that."

"Have we received any communications from FREN or TSA?" Frey asked.

"Nothing yet. I'll contact you as soon as we do."

"Thanks Slavin." Frey turned back to the door. "Let's go and visit my lab."

Einarr had a vague sense of already having passed through the passageways they now traversed on his earlier flight from the ice but was still unprepared for the sight of the smashed and broken glass and buckled metal doors.

"I did this?" He turned in a slow circle.

"Yeah," She sighed. "The security guard stationed outside this second door died in the blast."

"The ice screamed and groaned and I was suddenly catapulted outward. I started to run the moment I realized I was free and still alive."

She stepped through the debris and picked something up from the desk. "I'll take this back to my quarters in case FREN needs to contact me."

"Your quarters?" He smiled down at her.

She rolled her eyes. "Come on, and don't expect anything fancy. There isn't enough room to swing an Earth cat."

6

As she headed for her quarters, Frey was all too aware of the Viking pacing behind her. Luckily, he was tall so he could keep up with her. She should be embarrassed at how fast she was going, but she was beyond caring what anyone thought. She reached her cabin, punched in the codes and pushed open the door.

"This is my—"

They were the only word she got out before his mouth covered hers and he hauled her against his chest her back to the door. With a gasp, she surrendered to his possessive kiss and enthusiastically writhed against the hard planes of his chest and the glorious bulge of his shaft.

His hands worked on her uniform, shoving it down off her shoulders to uncover her breasts. She tried to undo his leather jerkin but couldn't work out how, so just continued to kiss him until he had her naked, her arms wrapped around his neck and her knees gripping his hips. With a deep growl, he unfastened his trews and then Gods...his stiff wet cock probed for entrance and she took him in, each thrust a welcome invasion, each thick inch of him parting her willing flesh.

She started to come before he'd even fitted himself totally inside her. With a grunt, he shifted one hand under her ass, hoisted her even higher and drove himself home and then again until she was whimpering and crying with the pleasure of being filled and fucked by a big strong man who could read her mind. Even as their bodies joined, so did their thoughts, enhancing the experience, blending them together into something else entirely.

She screamed into his mouth when she came again, and he froze and surrendered to her, his come pumping out in long thick waves until he started to shake with the force of it. When she felt him stagger, she pushed on his chest and guided him to fall back onto her small bed his cock still inside her.

Her cheek rested on his leather armor and she smiled as he cursed slowly in his own language, the words so guttural that the translator had no thoughts to offer as to their meaning.

She sat up making him groan and patted his chest.

"Take everything off. I want to see you."

He gave her a very slow and satisfied smile, his hands coming to rest on her hips.

"Help me, then."

He showed her how to unlace the leather garments and where they opened. Without the modern conveniences of tape and self-sealing fabrics, it took a long time to finally unwrap her male. But it was worth it.

Frey wondered if she was drooling as she revealed his broad chest, tight abs and muscular arms. And his cock... she couldn't wait to get her hands and mouth on him again.

"Be my guest." He murmured as she stroked one hand down over his stomach to the curve of his hip. His skin was pale and marked with several scars. She intended to kiss every single one.

"Not yet." He grabbed her hand and placed it on his cock. "I want you again, skin to skin."

She practically purred as he thrust his other hand into her hair and held her still until she leaned forward to kiss him. The tip of his cock brushed over her clit and she kept it there, using him to rub her most sensitive spot until he was as wet as she was and arching off the bed.

Shaking off his hands, she sat back and slowly lowered herself down over his thick shaft, relaying every sensation to him until she was fully seated on his impressive length. He took a deep breath making his stomach flex.

"Ride me, Frey. Make me yours."

She could barely hold his burning gaze as she eased up and then back down on him and then kept doing it as he shuddered beneath her. Faster now, and then his hand on her hip helping her, grinding her down onto his cock until she could think of nothing but him, his body, his mind and how he made her feel.

His fingers slid down over her hip until his thumb touched her clit and then she came so hard she had to close her eyes against the pleasure. It didn't matter. She couldn't hide from him. He knew what he was doing to her, had known it from the first moment she touched him.

She'd had sex with telepaths before, but it had never felt like this. This was truly life changing… His grip on her hip became more demanding as he set his feet flat on the bed and pumped up into her, meeting her half way like a bucking horse. He eased more upright, holding her steady and took her to another level of ecstasy she'd never realized existed, his mouth on her breasts as he strained upward to meet her.

"Frey…" he breathed her name like a prayer.

His climax made him hold her so tightly, she almost couldn't breathe. As she joined him with her mind and body, all the lights in her cabin shimmered and burnt out sending glass flying everywhere. She couldn't work out if the whole cabin structure was flexing or if it was just her bed.

"Tecky?" The banging on the door made her want to groan

in a different way. "Are you okay in there? The door locks jammed."

"We're fine," she yelled. "Don't come in, there's glass all over the floor. I'm going to clean it up."

"We need a visual on you, Tecky, right now. You and the Viking, copy?"

She knew Brown would break down the door if she didn't comply. With a curse, she grabbed her com device, wrapped her arm around Einarr's neck and pointed the viewfinder back at their flushed faces.

"See? We're fine. Now go away. If I need anything, I'll communicate with Slavin, okay?"

There was a snort of laughter; another bang on the door and then the noise went away. Frey lay back down, her head under the Viking's chin.

"We blew out the lights."

He kissed the top of her hair. "We don't need light."

"True, but we could end up getting cut to ribbons if we have to get out of bed."

"Why would you wish to do that?"

"To pee, or to take a shower maybe?"

"Ah." He held her close, his thumb stroking from neck to shoulder. "What is a shower? Like rain?"

"Kind of like an indoor waterfall."

His fingers stopped moving. "That's how we were trapped in the ice. Aki and I tried to cross through a cave behind an underground waterfall. We didn't make it to the other side." He sighed. "My grandfather told me it was an escape route. I didn't think he meant a magical one that would transport us into the future."

"Your family all had special powers?"

"Not all. Maybe one or two in each generation and always when there were twins."

"You and Aki are twins?"

"Aye." He settled her more comfortably against his shoulder so that she could look up at his face. "My family have been sorcerers and seers and wise men to the great families of the northern lands for centuries. Some of us also have the gift of reading each other's thoughts."

"We have a family like that on my planet, but all the seers are female. I believe the line has been unbroken for centuries."

"Your planet?"

"I'm from Pavlovan. It's closer to here than your planet Earth is."

He shook his head. "I still find the idea that my world is only one of many quite unbelievable. But here I am." He hesitated, his voice a deep rumble that vibrated his chest. "My world does still exist?"

"Sure it does. I was based there last year. That's why I got the opportunity to accompany you back to Alpha Three, seeing as I was going home anyway." It was her turn to sigh. "I think you'll find it changed beyond recognition."

"I thought as much."

Frey patted his chest. "There will be people on Alpha Three to help you through this. You and your brother are not the first people to be reborn into a different century. There was a fad on Earth for cryogenic freezing at the end of the twentieth century. Some of those people and body parts have been successfully revived."

"But no one as old as me and Aki."

"I don't think so." Frey came up on one elbow and studied her Viking's austere face. "They'll help you. They really are very good at what they do."

He regarded her for a long moment and then cupped her cheek. "You are kind."

"I'm…" She tried to smile. "I'm a complete free-fall mess at the moment. I have no idea what I'm doing, I certainly shouldn't be sleeping with you, and I'm definitely going to lose my job.

But I don't care. I couldn't keep away from you if I tried." She was obviously a lot more like her carefree committment-phobe father than she'd realized.

"Of course you couldn't stop yourself. We are fated to be together."

"Fated and mated." Frey whispered. Two different cultures and races separated by thousands of miles and years. Was it possible that they both meant the same thing?

"Are you okay with this?" She waved vaguely at her naked body, which was still entwined with his. "I can stop—"

"I can't" he rolled her onto her back and pushed her thighs wide with his knees. "Take me again."

When Einarr finally fell asleep, Frey untangled herself and switched on the emergency light on her com to survey the damage. Glass sparkled on the floor—the automatic cleaning system hadn't done its job and sucked away the debris. Crawling to the foot of her bunk, she placed her hand on the power control panel and used her telepathic abilities to sense the problems and repair the damaged fibers.

It didn't take more than a minute for the vacuum system to quietly come back online and clear the floor. She spent another moment reconnecting the lights and reinforcing both the door locks and the security precautions she'd put in place to secure the cabin from the rest of the ship. She'd probably get in trouble for that, too, but at this point, she was so far out of line that it hardly seemed to make much difference.

In the bathroom, she studied her face in the small mirror. Apart from some red patches of stubble burn on her throat, she looked exactly the same. Weird when her whole world had changed... She took a deep breath. It seemed she couldn't escape her genetics after all. Despite trying to live her life in a controlled, and quite frankly, boring manner she'd lost all sense of responsibility the moment she'd met Einarr.

Whatever happened in the future, she would never forget

her Viking and the gift he'd given her—the knowledge of what a true-mated pair felt and thought together. And, unlike her father, who had never intended to stay with her mother and just lied, she'd make sure that when Einarr left her she'd wave him goodbye with a smile and never let him know what he might have meant to her.

She bit her lip as her smile faded. When they reached Alpha Three, they'd be separated. She'd have to face her employers and he…would be facing months, if not years, of reintegration training. If his brother survived, at least he'd have someone to share the experience with. What would she have? A hurried dismissal and a transport back to Pavlovan if she was lucky. A public trial and prosecution if FREN were in a picky kind of mood.

But they'd given her the new codes… She'd just done what they'd told her to do. Which meant nothing. She'd touched the blood and added hers. She might be young, but she wasn't naïve. FREN wasn't known for its nurturing environment and any blame, especially if Einarr failed to survive, would fall squarely on her. They couldn't have known she'd find her mate, though. Would it make a difference if she told them? Would they let her stay with him? Somehow she doubted it.

She'd asked her grandmother once what it felt like when one of your mates died. She hadn't expected to make her cry. It seemed that even thirty years after the event, a mate was still mourned. And she would be losing hers before she could even publicly claim or acknowledge him. But she couldn't be selfish about this. Einarr deserved better.

He knew nothing about Pavlovan mating culture, and she refused to make a claim on him that he wouldn't understand or might accept because he didn't know any better. At her core, she wanted to own him, to make him hers, but knew that it would be selfish and wrong. She couldn't expect him to make promises he had no intention of keeping. He'd end up hating and resenting her. She'd rather stop before she got involved and hope he was left in blissful ignorance of what might have been. That was the practical, sane thing to do. The thing the *normal* her wouldn't think twice about.

With a sigh, she cleaned up and went back into the cabin. Her Viking lay sprawled on his back, one arm behind his head and one leg bent at the knee. She paused to study his magnificence. What was that quote her mother loved? Better to have loved and lost than never to have loved at all or something? She couldn't decide whether that was true or not. If she had her way, she'd fight with her bare hands to keep this male.

Her hands clenched into fists. She shouldn't have touched him. She'd never get over him now.

"There's no need to look so fierce, my female. Come back to bed."

She started as she realized he was watching her through narrowed eyes. How long did they have together before the ship landed up Alpha Three? Hours? Days? She had no idea. It was too late for regrets. She only knew that she would stay glued to his side for every second that was granted to her and try and forget what would happen after that.

***

EINARR WOKE up again and was relieved to see that Frey was still with him. In truth, because of the narrowness of the cot, she lay sprawled over him, her cheek on his chest and her thigh across his groin. He had no sense of time. The ship sped through darkness, which never seemed to end.

He sensed that she was troubled about something, but was unsure what it was. She'd tried to hold back her thoughts and her body from him during their last bout of lovemaking, and it wasn't that she was tired or sore. It was as though she was deliberately building a wall between them. Didn't she understand that he would never let her go? That he would fight and kill to keep her safe?

Perhaps things were different in her world, and mating with a man was always this powerful. That thought made him want to growl. She murmured something soothing against his chest and stroked his skin. He forced himself to settle down again. The ship hummed around them, its various sounds now familiar to Einarr and almost comforting. He thought of leaving the ship and finding out Aki's fate. Had his twin survived within the ice or had the "eclipse" affected him, too?

If Frey hadn't been with him, and he'd awakened by himself, would he still be alive? Her presence had soothed his fears and allowed him not to go into a blind panic at the strangeness of everything. If Aki woke up alone…

"What is it?"

She reached for him with her thoughts.

"I am wondering what has befallen Aki." He cleared his throat and spoke his fear out loud. "I hope the Gods have looked kindly upon him."

"Can you sense him?"

He opened his eyes and looked down at her. "How?"

She tapped his forehead. "With your thoughts."

"Aki is not as strong as I am magically. I'm not sure if he would hear me over such vast distances."

She came up on her elbows and leaned over him, her auburn hair tickling his skin.

"We could do it together." She paused when he didn't respond. "If you call him in your mind, I can add my telepathic strength, my thoughts, to yours."

He studied her earnest expression and the line of freckles that drifted over her nose. *"Show me."*

"Call his name. Shout it in your head." Her fingers encircled the pulse at his throat. *"That's right, now…"*

Her power flooded through him, sending Aki's name

booming out like Thor's hammer into the darkness. He waited but heard nothing except the echo of his own words.

She sighed and kissed him. "It's all right. We can try when we get closer to Alpha Three. It's possible that he avoided any effects from the eclipse and is still frozen in the ice."

"Or dead."

"Would you sense that?"

He shrugged. "I do not know. I do not know anything anymore."

She held his gaze. "I know that you are a strong man and that you will not let these strange and wonderful events break you."

Her confidence in him shamed him. With a groan he speared his fingers through her hair and brought her head down so that he could kiss her. Who needed words when he had this? A blood link with the female who had made sure of his survival.

"Your people are all magical?" he asked softly.

"Magical?" She smiled at him. "Not really. We are all telepaths, which means we can talk without using the spoken word just like you and Aki can. The only Pavlovan family I'd consider *magical* is that of the Oracle. She has powers beyond the norm."

"Does she use her power for the good of her people?"

"She foretells the future, and often finds Pavlovans their mates, which is pretty special."

"Ah, she has the sight." Einarr smoothed Frey's hair away from her cheek. "I wish I had that gift."

"Then you wouldn't be here with me now."

"I am glad to be with you, but still..." he hesitated. " I am afraid. I have no understanding of this place. I miss my home by the river and my family." He had to swallow hard as his voice thickened. Would she think him a coward? "I am nothing, here."

She cupped his cheek. "There is no shame in admitting you

are afraid. That takes courage." She kissed his nose. "If I'd woken up back in your time I'd be a raving lunatic by now."

"Or dead." He countered.

"Probably." Her hand traveled down from his neck to his armbands. "I have no magic to save me either." She traced the engraved marks. "These are runes aren't they? What do they say?"

"I cannot tell you the exact words because they are sacred. It is a prayer to Odin asking him to make me a channel for his power."

Her fingers lingered on his arm making all the fine hairs quiver to life.

"That's why the armbands glowed when you were fighting."

"Odin likes his servants to win."

Her expression became serious. "Don't tell them about your magic."

"Tell who?"

"The scientists on Alpha Three. Especially not the ones from your home planet, because they don't believe in magic anymore on Earth. They might tell FREN and you don't want them thinking of you as a potential weapon."

"Who is Fren? Is he your earl or king?"

"FREN is an organization with similar powers to those of a king. But they aren't good people, and they won't use you or your powers for good."

'But would they let me fight?"

"Not in the way you want. They'd take what they needed and you'd never be the same again."

He frowned as her voice broke.

"These people are your enemies? Do you want me to kill them for you?"

"That's very kind of you, but there are thousands of them. I just want you to be careful. I want you to survive."

He studied her carefully, aware of her bone deep concern for him. He touched her mouth. "Would you fight by my side like a shield maiden if Fren attacked us?"

She smiled. "I'd rather hide behind you. I'm not much of a fighter."

With some difficulty in the narrow cot, he rolled her onto her back and crouched over her, his knees pushing her thighs wide.

"I would protect you."

"I know."

She was beautiful, his woman. Her skin pale and her hair the reddish brown of an autumn leaf on the turn. Soft in all the right places, too, but with a core of strength and practicality that had helped her face him without fear and convince him to *live.* He kissed her again and then allowed his lips to move lower, feathering down her throat to her breasts, where her tight hard nipples awaited him. He took his time sucking them into his mouth and playing with them. She deserved to be worshipped and cherished.

"Your skin is so soft," he murmured.

She gave a shaky laugh. "Flatterer. You just haven't seen a woman for four thousand years. Anyone would look good."

He kissed her slightly rounded stomach. "No. Only you. I only wish to please you."

She moaned his name as he went lower, his tongue seeking and finding her already swollen bud, and lavishing it with attention until she grabbed hold of his head, her nails digging into his scalp, and shuddered through a climax. He smiled against her throbbing flesh and pointing his tongue pushed it deep into her channel and then out again mimicking the thrust of his cock. She was a little tender, but didn't seem to be holding herself back from him in any way.

"*Please...*"

"*Mmm?*" He kept up the slow advance and retreat of his

tongue as she started to writhe underneath him making it hard for him to breathe.

"Please fuck me."

"I am."

She gave a frustrated whimper that pleased him greatly. *"With your cock."*

He gave her one long last lick and then sat back on his heels and smoothed a hand over the stiffness of his wet shaft. *"This?"* He looked down at himself. *"Are you not sore?"*

"I don't care. I want you."

"Then you will have me."

She sighed as he eased the thick crown of his cock inside her. He rocked back and forth until she allowed him deeper and then deeper until he was fully sheathed inside her hot, slick sex.

He held himself still, allowing the beat of his heart to slow and match the throb of his cock. Taking his weight on one hand, he wrapped the other around both her wrists and drew her hands over her head. Her brown eyes widened as he stared down at her.

"When you are tired of taking me like this, will you let me have your mouth or your arse?"

She didn't falter. "Yes."

He slowly rocked his hips. "Have you taken a man like that before?"

"In my mouth, yes," she wiggled underneath him. "Do we have to talk about this now, couldn't you just—" She gasped as he moved a little faster. He liked her spread beneath him and impaled on his cock, liked the way her body trembled and swayed toward him, seeking more even when she was obviously tired.

"Did you like sucking a man's cock?"

She made a face. "Not particularly."

"You'll like sucking mine. I'd like to see you on your knees taking me into your mouth and making me come down your throat." His mind flowed into hers showing her how he pictured it, making her want it as much as he did. "I wouldn't force myself on you, you'd take me willingly, and beg for it."

She raised an eyebrow. "You're that good are you?"

"The skill will be yours. Seeing your lips around my shaft will probably kill me."

"How to bring a strong man to his knees..." she murmured.

"You would enjoy it." Her slight smile made him want to smile back at her. "And my cock in your arse, too."

Her cheeks reddened. "I haven't tried that."

"It is different, but it can be equally satisfying in its own way." He closed his eyes as her flesh tightened around his embedded cock. "You are harder to fuck there, but then I can also use my fingers in your cunt and clit."

"So I've heard. One of my sisters has two male mates, and she insists that having them together like that is the most amazing experience ever."

"Two men?" Despite himself, Einarr's hips started rocking back and forth and his cock slid in and out of her. He forced himself to slow down, to give her everything without pounding into her with all his might. He almost succeeded, except she was as aroused as he was. She started to come all around his cock, clenching and releasing him until he could do nothing but follow her over the edge and pump his seed deep within her.

He released her hands and sank down over her, his face buried in her neck, his cock still inside her. Her hand came up and stroked his unbound hair.

"You really are incredible, you know."

"I do my best to please."

"Oh, I'm pleased. Can't you tell?" She kissed him. "I just can't believe that you want me. I mean I'm nothing special. Slavin is a lot prettier than me and she's a telepath and—"

He slid his hand over her mouth. "You are mine."

She blinked and looked away from him. "*Don't say that.*"

"Why not? It is the truth." He removed his hand and stared down at her. "*I am yours. You know this.*"

She didn't correct him, and after a long moment she nodded. "We should get some sleep. Then we can go and find out when we'll arrive at Alpha Three."

7

———————

Frey kept her head high and her gaze level as she and Einarr entered the mess hall. Everyone was there, of course.

"Tecky." Brown nodded to her. "Good job at keeping the Viking occupied in your cabin for thirty-six Earth hours. Don't know how you managed it."

Beside Frey, Einarr went still, his pale blue gaze coming to rest on Brown.

"We're good Brown. How close are we to Alpha Three?" She tried to maneuver Einarr into a seat, but he refused to budge. "I assume FREN still hasn't been in contact, or else I would've heard."

"We've heard nothing," Slavin strolled over and smiled at Frey putting herself between Einarr and Brown. "Alpha Three is only a few hours away. We'll be preparing for landing fairly soon."

Heald came out of the small galley kitchen with a couple of plates on a tray. "Sit down, Viking. We're eating leftovers from the food stores. I've got eggs, pigcow and cheesera sandwiches for you both." He winked at Frey as he set the food on the table. "I bet you need your strength."

Frey contemplated crawling under the table. Was it that obvious that she and Einarr had spent their entire time alone fucking? From the way everyone was looking at them, she had to suspect it was. So much for her reputation as an uptight technician who never let her hair down…

"Where is Travis?" Einarr asked.

Slavin grimaced. "He's trying to contact Alpha Three to give them a heads up on our anticipated arrival time. There is still a lot of interference from the eclipse. It's proving hard to get through."

"I hope everything's okay down there." Frey said. "It's odd that we haven't been able to raise anyone on any channel."

"I know."

Slavin sat down beside Frey, and Einarr finally joined them, his gaze moving between her and Slavin.

"Do you believe our destination is unsafe?"

"I don't know." Frey reached for her sandwich suddenly realizing how hungry she was. "It's probably fine. As it's on one of the moons of Odin, it might have suffered a similar communications error to the one we had onboard ship."

Einarr ate his sandwich in two bites and shoved the plate away. "I want my weapons returned to me."

"You'll have to speak to Captain Travis about that." Slavin stood and pushed her chair in. "I'm going back to the bridge."

"We'll join you fairly soon." At the thought that their journey was about to end, Frey's appetite deserted her, and she passed the rest of the sandwich over to Einarr. He eyed her suspiciously but accepted her gift and ate it in seconds.

"When we've finished here and cleaned up my cabin, we need to go up to the bridge to prepare for our landing on Alpha Three."

Einarr nodded, his thoughts obviously elsewhere. "Will the captain give me my weapons back before we land?"

"I doubt it."

"But what if the base has been attacked?"

She stood up. "Apart from the odd spat between my people and the Etruscans, this section of space is mainly free of conflict. The only person who would attack the base would be your brother, so I don't think you'll be getting your weapons back."

He shrugged, his expression calm. "I don't need them." He flexed his fingers. "I have all the power I need."

"You promised not to use it on the ship."

"But not when we land." He shot her a hard blue stare. "Mark my words, Frey. If I need to defend you, or my brother, I will do so."

***

Einarr waited as patiently as he could for Frey to finish her preparations and get ready to disembark the ship. After packing her possessions and delivering her bags to the cargo hold, she took him back up to the bridge.

"We're going to sit here."

Einarr took the seat she indicated and watched as she buckled him in and then did the same to herself. In front of him, he could see the rest of the crew. Some of them were engaged in bringing the ship ever closer to a purple and black sphere straight ahead of them. Captain Travis was issuing orders, his voice calm, his gaze fixed forward.

"All crew. Landing procedures will commence in one minute." Slavin said. "Make sure you are in your approved seating. Thank you."

The engines under his feet changed tone and roared deeper now, making the floor tremble and the upcoming planet tip alarmingly to one side. He fought back a desire to puke by swallowing hard and grabbed the armrest of his chair. Just as he did, a coil snaked out from behind his neck and wrapped itself around his throat and then into his ear and nose. He jerked forward with a growl.

"Don't fight it, Einarr. It won't hurt you. It's just a precautionary safety measure in case the ship loses life support."

Frey had obviously anticipated his desire to rip out the coiled wire and wrestle the thing to the ground. He tried to relax as the ship maneuvered again and came back toward the planet at some speed. Closing his eyes and praying seemed like the best option available, so he did that. Slavin's voice continued to talk softly in his ear as she guided the ship in, communicating with someone on the ground at every step.

He kept his eyes closed, even when the noise diminished and he felt the bump of solid ground beneath him, and breathed a prayer to the Gods.

"Ship is secured. Safety devices will deactivate in thirty seconds," Slavin said. "Captain Travis requests that Tecky stay with our guest and disembark last."

"Copy that." Frey said.

He remained in his seat until the web of wires retreated and he surreptitiously rubbed his throat. The crew filed out glancing curiously at him and smiling at Frey who didn't say a word. At last, only he, Frey, and Captain Travis were left on the bridge. He wished he had his weapons. He had a sense that his welcome might not be as benign as Frey expected.

Travis came over, his expression guarded.

"Science Officer Frey, fall in behind me and the Viking and proceed to the docking bay."

"Yes, sir."

Einarr held out his hand. "Where are my weapons?"

"They have already been taken off the ship. I'm sure the personnel at Alpha Three will return them to you when they deem you sufficiently rehabilitated."

"I would prefer to have them now."

Travis sighed. "There is nothing to fear here, Viking. No one wants to hurt a hair on your head. You are a scientific miracle. Trust me. They want to keep you alive."

Frey touched his sleeve. "He's right, Einarr. No one will harm you."

"Then we will proceed."

He followed Travis down the narrow passageways, his feet sounding hollowly on the metal until he reached a square of light. Bracing himself, he took a step outside and immediately covered his eyes against the brightness beaming down on him. He stopped dead and Travis paused beside him. A soft breeze blew up stirring the purple dust that covered the floor. The air was hot and dry and stuck in his throat.

"Keep moving, Viking." Travis murmured. "Nothing to worry about."

Despising himself for his moment of weakness, and even more that Travis had witnessed it, Einarr took a step forward. At the bottom of the ramp, a group of people awaited them. They were all staring at him and some of them were whispering excitedly. Raising his chin, he strode toward them, his gaze fixing on the woman at the front of the group who appeared to be in command.

She came toward him, her expression serene and held up her hand.

"Welcome, Einarr Bloodaxe, to Alpha Base Three. I'm Doctor Pel Aziz."

He took her measure, his hand hovering at his hip where his axe should be.

"Is my brother here?"

"Your brother?" Her eyebrows shot up. "The other warrior is related to you?"

"Aye, we are twins. Is he here?"

"His ship hasn't arrived yet. We expect it within the next few hours." She glanced over her shoulder at the huddle of curious faces. "We would like to examine you and make sure you haven't suffered too many ill effects since…"

"I came out of the ice." Einarr finished the sentence for her. "I am willing to cooperate until my brother arrives. And then I need to see him."

"As you wish." She hesitated. "We lost contact with his ship around the same time as we lost contact with yours and haven't reestablished it yet. We were only aware of your presence because Captain Travis managed to get a message through to us just before landing. We have no idea if your brother, um, defrosted as well."

"I'm sure that will become clear when he arrives." Einarr bowed, aware of the armed guards now moving in between him and Travis. "Where is Frey?"

Travis touched his shoulder. "She is being debriefed by her employers. I'm sure she'll join you later."

He shook off Travis's restraining hand, aware that he could no longer sense Frey in his head. "That is unacceptable. I need to—" A cold stabbing pain in his neck silenced him and even as he inwardly raged, he fell forward into the waiting arms of the soldiers who surrounded him.

FREY SAT down at the table again and rested her head on her folded arms. She'd been left to stew in the "interview" room for hours. When she'd tried the door, a uniformed guard had gotten in her face and told her to sit down and shut up or he wouldn't be responsible for his actions.

She groaned into her hands. This was bad. She couldn't even sense Einarr, and after seeing him keel over like a stunned ox, as she was marched away, she wasn't surprised. When he woke up and found her gone, would he care? Or would all his focus be on reclaiming his brother? She almost hoped it would. She didn't want to drag him into her mess. There was nothing she could do to help him and nothing he could do to make the coming ordeal about her failure to obey orders any better.

She'd never been in trouble in her life before. She'd obeyed every rule and done everything perfectly and she'd still ended up here... What did they say about her? Was she genetically engineered to break the rules? And Gods, her heart was breaking as she yearned to stay with her male and simply shut everything else out.

The door finally opened and she sat up straight as a man and woman entered the room and took the two seats opposite her at the table. The male wore the standard blue uniform of a TSA operative, the female civilian clothing, most of which was tight and shiny.

"Science Officer Frey. I'm Gron from the Trios Space Authority and this is my colleague Director Mitzi Lahm from FREN."

Frey nodded at the pair and resumed her contemplation of her folded hands. She hadn't quite expected Mitzi to look like that. FREN ops tended to be rather more uptight in their dress code.

"We've been asked to investigate your conduct aboard TSA Ship QZ41."

"I did what I was ordered to do." Frey said. "I kept the Viking alive."

"That is correct, but you were also instrumental in setting him free in the first place." Mitzi snapped. "You went directly against FREN procedure in ensuring the ice remained in a sterile environment."

"I followed the orders I was given *by* FREN and input only the codes that were sent to me."

"Codes you *conveniently* say you were told to erase."

"I was ordered to erase them. I'm fairly certain you'll find the information if you check the full security logs."

"You touched the ice with your bare hands."

It didn't appear as if Mitzi was listening or had any intention of replying directly to Frey's answers.

Frey shrugged. "Only once, and that was during an emergency. When the planets aligned, the—"

"I'm not interested in excuses, Science Officer," Mitzi made a slashing gesture with her hand. "You didn't follow protocol."

"I was more concerned about keeping your specimen alive. As soon as the eclipse sent all my equipment into a spin, I checked the Viking. I didn't have time to worry about gloves when the whole ship's power might have been failing." Frey took a quick breath and kept talking. "And if anything was to blame for the defrosting, I think you should look at the effect of the new codes you sent me and at the eclipse. When was the last time these planets, including ones called after the Viking gods aligned? I bet that has more to do with it than me sticking one naked finger on the surface of the ice."

"Those particular circumstances are being fully investigated, Science Officer Frey. We are more concerned with your decision making process throughout the entire voyage," Gron said. "You took it upon yourself to keep the Viking with you at all times."

"The Viking suggested it. He threatened to destroy the ship if I didn't comply."

"So Captain Travis said." Gron sat back. "But even if that is correct, I'm sure no one suggested you have sexual relations with this man."

Frey felt her cheeks heat up. "Captain Travis did not ask me to do that. It just… happened."

Mitzi slammed her hand down on the table. "And it is completely unacceptable! How *could you* be so unprofessional? You have no idea how his body has withstood being trapped in ice for centuries. You have no idea what diseases he carries, or what you might have given him."

Frey bit down on her lip and stared at the table. She wasn't going to bring out the mating excuse. There was no way she and Einarr could ever be together now. Suggesting that she was his mate would open up a whole new can of worms that Einarr didn't need and her interrogators wouldn't understand.

"Well?" Mitzi demanded.

Frey shrugged. "I wanted to keep him safe."

"By letting him have unprotected sexual intercourse with you?" Mitzi shook her head. "You might just have killed him before he even had a chance to live again. How selfish and thoroughly unprofessional of you."

Well, she had been selfish. Frey knew that, but she didn't regret experiencing sex with a telepathic mate. It was extraordinary. But had she damaged him? She hadn't sensed anything wrong with him, and mates were attuned to physical changes in their lover's bodies. In fact, they were more likely to heal each other than to cause harm.

Oh Gods, was she such a screw-up that one moment of spontaneity and selfishness in her entire life might have killed her mate?

"I did what I thought best to keep him alive and safe." She repeated the words gaining some comfort from them. "If that means I should resign my commission and return to Pavlovan, then I'll do so right now."

Mitzi sat back. "Don't think you'll get off that easily, Science Officer. Have you any idea how much money FREN invested in this project?"

Frey looked Mitzi right in the eye. "Sure I do, but maybe you should be thanking me. You'll save a fortune because he's already defrosted. Although I didn't cause that, I *did* follow orders and keep him alive."

Gron nodded. "You did. Captain Travis agrees with that at least."

"I appreciate Captain Travis's support," Frey said tightly.

After a quick glance at each other, Mitzi and Gron rose to their feet.

"We will continue this conversation after the Viking has cleared his initial health assessments. If he *doesn't* clear them, we will require your presence in the medical lab."

"To do what?" Frey looked up when Mitzi finished speaking.

"To be tested yourself. Until then you'll be held in custody by security."

"This is ridiculous." Frey scowled at the female. "The Viking is here, and he's in one piece, largely due to me. I understand that you have to follow protocol and that you need someone to blame for his defrosting. Just let me resign from my post and go home."

"You will not be allowed to leave Alpha Three until we have completed our inquiries." Mitzi turned and banged on the door. "If you are deemed to have breached your contract with FREN or TSA, you will be prosecuted."

"Great," Frey muttered as her two inquisitors went out to be replaced by four huge guards. "Not even one com call home? Or the Pavlovan ambassador to talk to? At least a word with *someone* who might understand and protect me?"

"Come with us, Science Officer Frey."

She checked out the guards and realized she had no choice but to do as she'd been told. All she could hope was that Einarr was safe and that he wasn't worrying about her at all. That would be for the best. Her chest tightened as if her heart was being squeezed tight. She refused to give in to the desire to cry. She had a sense that she would need all her strength to stand up to whatever was going to happen next.

Eventually, after walking through what felt like miles of corridors, she was gently maneuvered through a thick metal door into a small windowless cell. The door was locked before she even had time to turn around. With a sigh, she sank down onto the side of the small bed and shoved her fingers into her hair, loosening the braid.

She searched for Einarr in her mind but there was nothing, only a cold empty space where his thoughts should have been filling her. He wasn't dead. She would have known if he was, but he definitely wasn't conscious. Tentatively, she reached out to the only other Pavlovan she knew.

"Slavin?"

"Tecky, Are you okay? The whole crew has been detained at the base, and is being interviewed one by one. We have no idea what's going on."

"I'm sorry about that, but I'm not surprised. They are probably looking for evidence to use against me. I also doubt FREN wants a bunch of you wandering around the galaxy telling stories about a defrosted Viking right now."

"I had the same thought. I wonder if they'll force a memory erasure for the whole crew?"

Frey shuddered. For a Pavlovan, the TSA's casual attitude to wiping sensitive data from their population's minds was considered barbaric. It was also hugely damaging to telepaths. Everyone knew that the TSA tended to do a mind sweep first and deal with the inevitable claims from outraged citizens afterward. If said citizen hadn't gone crazy…

"Have you seen Einarr?" Frey couldn't help but ask.

"No." Slavin hesitated. *"They knocked him out and took him to the medical wing. I don't think they will let me see him."*

"I'm certain they won't let me see him. I've been locked up in the high security wing."

"Have you told them that you are mated to the Viking?"

"I didn't see the point. It's not as if they are going to let me stay with him or anything." Tears pricked behind Frey's eyelids and she resolutely swallowed them down. *"It's better for him if he doesn't have to deal with me while he is rehabilitated."*

"I don't think he'd agree with you."

"He doesn't have much choice. Neither of us do."

"Still... If I do see Einarr I'll tell him that you've been detained."

"Don't. I don't want him to think he has to rescue me or anything." Frey took a steadying breath. "There is something you can do for me, though."

"What is it?"

"Find out if there is a government representative from Pavlovan on this base and tell them about me. Tell them everything."

"Done. Anything else?"

"Check and see when the last time these planets aligned? I bet it was around four thousand Earth years ago when Einarr and his brother were first trapped in the ice."

"I'll do my best." Slavin paused. "I have to go now. It's my turn to be interviewed. Wish me luck."

8

EINARR OPENED HIS EYES AND STARED UP AT YET ANOTHER WHITE ceiling. He was bound to the bed and he couldn't move anything but his fingers and toes.

"Oh good, you are awake."

There was a whirring sound, and his pallet suddenly rose at an angle until he was almost vertical but still strapped to the bed. The healer, Aziz, who had welcomed him to the base, stood beside him, her bright blue uniform now covered with a white coat.

He fixed her with his most intimidating glare. "I am getting tired of being knocked out, tied up and treated like an animal of low worth."

She had the grace to look ashamed. "I am sorry about that. We wanted to get as many of the medical unpleasantries accomplished as possible while you were unconscious."

He became aware of a myriad of small irritations on his skin, as if he'd been eaten alive by a swarm of biting insects. His head felt as if he'd received another blow from an axe.

"Where is my brother?"

"His ship hasn't landed yet. It is expected within the hour."

"Then I wish to be free to greet him."

She sighed. "We'll do our best. We're still waiting on test results."

"I do not care what you are waiting for. I want to see my brother."

"If he's survived as well as you have, you'll be seeing plenty of him. The pair of you will need to enter a program of extensive rehabilitation."

Einarr ignored that. "Where is Frey?"

"Science Officer Frey?" Aziz's expression sharpened. "Why do you want to know?"

He raised an eyebrow. "Because she is of my blood."

"I'm not sure I get your meaning."

"Frey belongs with me. Where is she?"

"I *believe* she's still here on the base."

"I know that." Einarr said impatiently. "She needs to be here with me."

"Why?"

"She is my *female*. Her blood called me to her through the centuries."

Aziz cocked her head to one side. "Do you really believe that?"

"How could I not?"

She wrote something down on her white slate. "How do you know Science Officer Frey is still on the base? Do you smell her blood or something?"

He remembered too late Frey's warning to him about not sharing his powers. "You talk to me as if I am a beast hunting his prey. Let me free. I will find Frey and my brother."

"I can't let you go until I've been given the okay by FREN and the TSA." She patted his arm. "Let me go and check on those test results. I'll be right back."

She showed him how to lower and raise his bed and some other things and then went out with a cheery wave. Einarr felt an unaccustomed slow rage build within him like a fire licking at a thatched roof. Someone had removed all his clothing and his arm rings leaving him in a thin blue shroud like garment that barely reached his knees. He took a moment to observe the nature of the webbing binding him to the bed and then concentrated his magic. There was a horrible burning smell, but his bonds refused to break.

Nonplussed, he tried again, but he was still trapped. Reining in his anger, he took a deep breath and focused on Frey. Her shields were up, guarding her thoughts, but they were no match for him.

"Frey."

"Einarr, oh thank Gods, are you okay? Have they hurt you?"

He wanted to smile at the raw emotion in her voice. *"I am well. I will come to you soon."*

Silence.

"You...don't have to do that. I'm fine. You focus on helping your brother. He's going to need you."

Einarr frowned. *"I will of course help Aki, but I will also find you."*

"There's no need."

He felt as if someone had punched him hard in the guts. *"Frey, I..."*

He jumped as the glass light over his door flashed red and started wailing like a thousand howling wolves. He couldn't even cover his ears. A voice bellowed out.

"All security teams to the docking bay. All security teams to the docking bay."

The dock must be where he'd landed and where Aki was expected. Einarr glanced at the door and then pushed the button Aziz had shown him how to use if he wanted help. No one came. After another few seconds, he forced another pulse of magic through his bound wrists, causing more of the foul smell and a slight softening of the rope-like substance. With an almighty roar, he wrenched his arms free, ripping through the restraints and set to work on his ankles.

Wedging the chair against the door, he searched the room and found his belongings stacked neatly on a shelf in the cupboard. There was still no sign of his weapons. Dressing quickly, he moved the chair back against the wall and peered out of the door. The hall was deserted, as if the screech of the alarm had driven everyone away.

FREY JUMPED up as the security alarms started blaring and sensed the guards outside her door moving away. Sticking her fingers in her ears she walked over to the door, reached above it and managed to shut the alarm up.

"Einarr? Did you hear that? It's an alarm. It should stop in a moment."

She leaned against the door awaiting his response. If the alarm had scared her, what had Einarr made of it?

"I am well, Frey. I believe Aki's ship has been sighted. I'm going to see what is happening down at the docks. Can you join me there?"

Frey thought he sounded remarkably calm considering. *"I don't think so. I'm locked up."*

"Then I will find you when I've dealt with Aki."

"It's okay. I'll try and get out of here myself. You don't have to worry about me."

"I will find you, Frey, regardless."

She was torn between gratitude at his obvious sincerity and fear that he meant it. *"Be careful."*

He snorted. *"I will do my best. I assume they will be reluctant to kill me until I have paid for my journey here."* He paused. *"If you plan to escape, mayhap you could find my weapons and bring them with you?"*

"Sure, why not?" She grimaced at her slightly hysterical response.

"Now I just have to find my way back to the docks," Einarr continued speaking. *"It is hard to read most of these symbols on the walls."*

"Oh that's easy." Frey said, pulling up the map of the base in her head and relaying it to him. *"Go to level 01 and look for a symbol that resembles three inverted 'v's like the head of an arrow. That's the sign for the docking bays. Aki's ship will be coming in to one of those. It will be pretty obvious which one it is if the entire Alpha Three military is surrounding it."*

His laughter saturated his thoughts, and for a moment, she forgot to hold him at arm's length and simply enjoyed being so in tune with him. It wasn't fair for him to have to face the might of Alpha Three all by himself. She put her hand on the control panel on the wall of her cell.

"I'll try and join you."

The security system hadn't banked on a Pavlovan's telepathic ability to disrupt electrical patterns and currents. It was a flaw she was more than happy to exploit. She'd already lost her job, and her future was in doubt. What was to stop her helping the Viking? If she was being screwed by FREN, Gods knew what they planned to do to an ancient Viking.

Letting out a slow breath, she placed her hand back on the control panel and focused on the intricacies of the security system until she understood the flow well enough to reach in and telepathically disrupt it. Her cell door lock clicked open, and with a soft prayer, she eased it open an inch until she could see out onto the corridor. There was no one there, only the flashing red lights, the boom of the alarm, and the sound of hurried orders being issued over the public com.

If Einarr's weapons were on Alpha Three, they would be stored in the most secure area, which had to be where she was currently being held. As she ran along the corridor, she used the matrix of the building plans to identify exactly where she was.

"Einarr? This might sound weird, but can you connect with your weapons at all? I mean magically or telepathically?"

From the stream of his thoughts, she could tell he was also on the move, his route downward through a series of emergency staircases and locked doors.

"Aye, I can sense they are here."

"Can you send that thought to me?"

For a moment, he went quiet, and she considered how to rephrase her request. She'd grown up surrounded by telepaths and never had to think about how she'd acquired her knowledge. Trying to explain things to a four-thousand-year-old Viking was proving to be a lot more complicated than she'd anticipated.

She almost gasped as the image of his axe and dagger appeared in her mind with such vivid clarity that she wanted to reach out and touch them.

"Hold that thought, Einarr. Call them to us."

He understood her better than she had anticipated, his strength blending with hers and leading her unerringly to a manned desk at the center of the small detention center. Frey thanked her Gods that Alpha Three was a research complex and not a military base as the lone man stared at her, consternation on his face. He looked about sixteen-years-old and everything about him screamed research geek.

"How the hell did you get out?"

She blinked innocently at him. "My door opened when the alarm went off. I assumed I was *supposed* to get out?"

"I…"

"Perhaps you should go and ask someone?" She checked his nametag. "Merton, is it? I'm quite happy to wait here while you check."

He stared at her and then tapped his wrist com. "Pastur? Come in, please. We have a situation here."

Half turning his back on her, he repeated the request. It was just enough time for Frey to lean forward, grab the weapon he'd left on the desk, and point it at him.

"Stop talking, Merton, and turn off your com."

He swallowed hard. "You can't do this. What's the point? Someone will just get hurt."

"Turn it off."

She kept the weapon pointed at his head until he shut down his com. "I won't hurt you if you tell me where you've stored the Viking's weapons."

His gaze flicked nervously toward the door behind him. "I can't tell you that. It is classified information."

"Oh for goodness sake," Frey huffed. "The weapons are totally harmless in this society and they belong to our *guest*. If the other Viking has defrosted and gone berserk on that space ship then *our* Viking might be the only person who can calm him down."

"Well he won't need his weapons for that."

"He *might*. It would be unfair of him to use a modern weapon on his own kin, wouldn't it?"

Merton bit his lip. "I still don't like it."

"You don't have to like it. You can just tell your superiors that I held a gun on you and forced you to get the weapons for me. You'll be a hero."

"I doubt that."

"You're not military, are you? No one will expect you to do anything *violent*," Frey said reassuringly. Part of her wanted to stand back and appreciate the absurdity of their conversation while the rest of her was desperate to move on and help Einarr. She hardened her resolve. "I don't *want* to use this weapon, but I will if I have to."

He sighed. "I'm an intern on a science scholarship. I don't want all this hassle. I'll get you his weapons."

"Thank you."

"Turn your back so you don't see the codes I'm inputting."

Frey fixed him with her most intimidating stare. "Yeah, right. I'm a Pavlovan I can probably do it myself. Just go ahead. I promise not to tell anyone." She could take over at this point, but she didn't have to. It might be worth informing Alpha Three that any Pavlovan over the age of five would stand a good chance of breaking through their power systems and that they might want to fix that. But not quite yet...

Merton came back clutching two large sealed packages to his chest. "I think these are the weapons."

As soon as she ripped off the wrapping and touched the first item Frey knew she held another powerful source of Einarr's magic. The handle of the axe was worn smooth and the dark grey blade pitted with tiny nicks and scratches. The second weapon was a long dagger within a leather sheath. Tossing the plastic aside, she winked at Merton and took off at a run toward the docks.

She thought she heard him call out, demanding the return of *his* weapon, and she pretended not to hear. Einarr might be proficient with an axe and dagger, but she certainly wasn't. She suspected he might need all the help modern weaponry could provide.

<hr>

EINARR CROUCHED behind a large pile of barrels and scanned the area around the dock. Lights flashed and sirens blared, but the place appeared to be deserted. A ship that looked like the twin of the one he'd arrived on sat on the ground, heat still vibrating in waves off the metal surface. The high-pitched whining sound of what Frey had called the engines reminded him of a million angry honeybees in full swarm. The main door stood open and a single body lay stretched out on the gangplank.

"Come out with your hands up."

Einarr jumped as a magnified voice echoed over the docking bay.

"We will not harm you."

Another slight movement behind him had him whirling to face Brown, the security guard from the ship he'd arrived on. Brown jammed his weapon against Einarr's throat and leaned in close pointing to the open door.

"I think your brother's awake. He appeared at the door and threw the body out. There's no apparent way to communicate with the ship's crew or him."

Einarr frowned. "Mayhap they were unable to give him the necessary tools to translate your language."

"It's highly likely. We were lucky that you were distracted enough by Frey for her to put the translator on you." Brown glanced to the side. "I'm fairly sure you shouldn't be here, but I reckon you are the only chance we have to get out of this without a bloodbath."

"What do you expect me to do? Go in there and kill him for you?"

"As if you would." Brown shifted his position. "I'm more interested in preventing a massacre of innocent scientists who've definitely bitten off more than they can chew with you two guys. The security on this planet sucks ass, and they are already panicking. I don't want you or your brother to die."

Einarr stared into the other man's eyes judging his worth. "Then I will help you."

"Good." Brown withdrew his weapon. "Just remember if you try anything fancy, I have the ability to blow your brains out with one click of my finger."

Even as he finished speaking he stiffened as Frey appeared

on his other side and held a weapon on him. Einarr smiled at her.

"My lady."

Not taking her eyes off Brown who was cursing quietly, she grinned at Einarr. "I've got your weapons."

"Thank you." He nodded at Brown. "You can lower your weapon, Frey. We will help him."

He waited until she stowed her weapon and then she carefully handed over his axe and dagger to him. He couldn't help but smile as his fingers closed around the well-remembered grooves of the oak handle of his axe. He returned his dagger and sheath to his belt and kept hold of his axe.

"So what's the panic?" Frey asked. "I assume Aki is awake?"

"Awake and angry by the sound of it," Brown said. "The main power and com links on the ship are down. Aki's already thrown out one body. When he appeared the second time, he had the captain by the throat."

Frey looked at Einarr. "Can you reach him?"

He grimaced. "Aki's powers are not as strong as mine. I can hardly sense him at all. He is not acting in a rational way."

"Well, *duh*," Frey rolled her eyes.

He didn't understand the words, but her meaning was clear. Her ability to make fun of him even in the most dire of circumstances alternatively amused and befuddled him.

"I suspect I will have to go on the ship and find him myself."

"Not on your own." Brown stated.

"I thought you trusted me." Einarr raised an eyebrow. "It's hardly likely my brother and I will steal your ship and fly away. We do not have the ability."

"But you could force the crew to do it for you."

"I'll go with him." Frey said. "I can communicate with all sides. I'll slap a translator on the guy as soon as I get the chance."

Brown looked down at Frey. "How the hell did *you* get out anyway? And who gave you his weapons?" He shook his head.

"This security system is as full of holes as a slice of Swiss cheese. I've assumed command. I'll tell everyone what you two plan to do and stop any arguments." He turned to Frey. "Tecky, you need to keep me informed at all times."

"I will if my com works. Is Slavin around? She's Pavlovan. I can communicate telepathically to her."

Brown grimaced. "Then get her down here. The more the merrier."

9

EINARR WENT UP THE SLOPE TOWARD THE OPEN DOOR OF THE SHIP and paused beside the unmoving body of the man. Keeping a wary eye out for Aki, he went down on his knee and tried to find some sign of life within the slumped form. He breathed a prayer of thanks when he caught the faintest of heartbeats. If Aki hadn't actually killed anyone, it would make things a lot easier for them both.

Frey knelt beside him, her brown gaze locked on his.

"He's still alive." Einarr murmured. "Get Brown to take him to the healers after we go inside."

"Okay."

He stood offering Frey his hand, the other he kept on the shaft of his axe. Come."

For a moment she just stayed where she was and stared into his eyes before hurriedly turning away and following him into the darkness. It took a moment for his gaze to adjust to the dim lighting. He paused just inside the door as his boots crunched over something scattered all over the floor.

"*What's happened?*" he asked.

"*I suspect Aki blew the lights out. Let's just be thankful that's all he did. The ship automatically switches to back-up power to supply the emergency lighting that runs at floor level.*" She pointed downward. "*We're walking on broken glass. Can you sense where your brother is?*"

Einarr concentrated hard. "*Is this ship laid out in the same way as yours?*"

"*They are almost identical.*"

"*Then I think he's in the food hall.*"

Frey touched his arm. "*While we approach, try and block your thoughts from him. Can you do that?*"

"*I've never tried to shield my thoughts from Aki. There has never been a need.*"

"*I'd like to see if we can pick up anything from him—anything that might help us know how to deal with him.*"

"*Aye.*" Einarr focused inward, mirroring Frey's actions, and built a sturdy wall in his mind enclosing her with him and keeping everyone else, including Aki, out. It felt surprisingly secure. "*I sense his rage and fear. He believes he is alone and that he has nothing to live for.*" He started jogging faster. "*We don't have much time.*"

He remembered that the food hall had more than one entrance, which made things easier. It could be accessed from the kitchen, and there were two other doors, one at each end that went back into the main passageway.

"*Kitchen?*" He looked down at Frey who had already drawn her weapon.

"*Sure, I'll go through the back, while you grab his attention from the front. I'll shoot him with a tranquilizer dart and slap a translator on his ass so that we can start this conversation again.*"

"*That thing won't kill him?*" He gestured at her weapon.

"*Not this one. I have a proper gun in my belt, but I'm hoping I won't need to use it.*"

They were outside the kitchen door now. Frey smiled up at him. "*Good luck.*"

In response, Einarr slid his fingers into her hair and cupped her scalp bringing her up on tiptoe to kiss him. When she sighed and relaxed against him, he had to fight himself to end the kiss.

"*Wait for me to get into position.*" Einarr kissed her again.

She stepped back, her fingers to her mouth, her eyes wide and nodded.

He didn't want to leave her, but he could already hear voices from the food hall and knew Aki was in trouble. His mate could wait for his full attention. His brother could not.

FREY CREPT forward through the cold metal storage bins, the still warm ovens and the broken cups and plates until she was kneeling below the open serving hatch. Someone in the mess hall was crying softly and being comforted in a low-voiced murmur. A lone voice was talking and talking as if convinced that the Viking would at some point suddenly be able to understand what he was saying if he just kept getting louder.

Frey felt in her pocket for the translation patch. Why didn't the ship carry them? It was a fairly standard piece of equipment. Or maybe the Viking had torn off the strip before it had become fully functional. She also checked the tranquilizer dart was armed and ready to go.

"*I can see him.*" Einarr said. "*He has his dagger at the captain's throat. Five men are tied up on the floor and three women are huddled together beside them. They all seem to be alive.*"

"*Good, that's pretty much the whole crew. Let me relay that to Slavin.*"

Einarr spoke again. "*I'm going to walk out in front of him, with my weapon held out and speak to him.*"

"*Are you sure that's the best approach?*"

"*I can think of no other.*"

"*You could wait, and I could see if I—*"

"Nay."

She fought a desire to curse his stubbornness as the swing door opposite the kitchen creaked and opened to reveal Einarr. While everyone's attention switched toward him she raised herself onto her knees so that she could see over the counter. With as much care as she could manage, she rested her elbows on the top, the tranquilizer gun held steadily between her hands. Aki's back was toward her and Einarr was moving forward, his axe held high.

"Aki? It's me, your brother, Einarr."

"Einarr?"

That was the only word Frey understood as the fair-haired Viking started screaming in ancient Norse.

"Nay, I am not a ghost or a vision from Valhalla. I am as alive as you are." Einarr said calmly. "Let the man go, lay down your weapon, and I will explain what has happened to you."

"Hvaða helvítis fáviti ertu!"

Had Aki just called his brother an idiot? It didn't seem to disturb Einarr's calm at all. Frey's grip on the dart tightened.

"We are both alive, Aki. Please, listen to me."

Aki shook his head as Einarr took three steps closer. There was another sharp exchange. The smell of blood caught at Frey's senses and a line of red dripped off the bone handle of Aki's dagger. His captive moaned a prayer.

Einarr continued to advance, his hand held out, and his expression calm. "I would never deceive you. I am your twin. Find me in your heart and mind, brother, hear my truth."

Frey added her power to Einarr's as he lowered his barriers and pushed deep into Aki's mind. He took another step forward, his gaze intent. Frey climbed up onto the countertop and took up her new firing stance.

"Aki…"

With a roar, Aki threw the captain to one side and launched himself at his brother, his dagger raised.

Frey yelled and threw herself off the counter coming down on Aki's back and shooting the tranquilizer dart directly into his neck. He fell forward with a snarl of pain. Even before he hit the ground, Einarr was on top of him, securing his hands behind his back.

He glanced up at Frey who had also rolled to one side. "You have the translator?"

She secured it to the back of Aki's neck, smoothing out the band until it was stuck firmly in place. If he wanted to remove it, he'd have to use a knife. Not that she thought that would stop him. She hoped he'd remain quiet long enough to understand that the translator wouldn't harm him. He was a big man like Einarr and he'd already started to regain consciousness. This time some of his curses were even translatable.

Einarr removed his brother's weapons and remained beside him, one hand smoothing his twin's fair hair away from his face.

"I'll watch him, Frey. Help untie the crew."

The females had also started on that task so the others were soon released and proved to be mainly unharmed. As she worked to free them, Frey heard several versions of the story. Apparently since the eclipse, Aki had picked them off one at a time, starting with the science officer assigned to care for him on the journey, and progressing through the crew until only the pilot and captain had been spared to do their job and land the ship.

After informing Brown that the situation was clear and he should get the medics onboard, Frey turned her attention to tracking down the science officer and comparing notes. If her opposite number had been the first to go down, it was highly likely that any special orders from FREN with regards to the Viking had not been carried out. After speaking to the shaken male, she discovered that had proved to be the case. Once he realized that his report and Frey's described similar occurrences related to the eclipse and the orders he'd received, he promised to send her a copy. She could only hope that it would prevent FREN from insisting everything that had happened was her fault.

"Frey?"

She looked around to see Aki being strapped on a gurney. His eyes were closed and he was breathing normally. His hair was the color of golden corn and was tied back in a braid like his twins. Einarr stood next to him, his blue gaze icy and fixed on her.

"What's up?"

"Come with Aki and me."

"Sure." She knew he wasn't pleased at her for literally leaping to his defense, but she wasn't going to sit still while Aki gutted her male on the end of his dagger. The fact that she hadn't even had to think about her decision to protect Einarr was unnerving. The gurney moved off, surrounded by a secure guard and followed by Einarr and Frey.

When they emerged into the docking bay, it looked like the whole of Alpha Three was present including an unhappy looking Dr. Pel Aziz and the reps from FREN and TSA.

"Oh *heeze*," Frey muttered. "Now we're in for it."

Dr. Aziz held up her hand blocking the others.

"Infirmary first for *everyone*. Questions later. No arguments."

FREY WAITED as Aki was sedated more heavily and the medical team converged on him to complete their assessments. Brown had secured the entire medical wing, and only she and Einarr were allowed anywhere near the unconscious Viking. She'd expected to be put back in her cell, but for some reason, no one had attempted to restrain her—yet.

She rolled her shoulders, aware of a number of aches and

pains collected during her adventurous day. Brown came out of Aki's room escorting a furious-looking Einarr.

"He's not going anywhere, Viking. Let the medical team get their tests done, okay?"

Einarr glared at him. "Get me the moment he awakens."

"I'll make sure that happens." Brown pointed at the room across the hallway. "Why don't you crash in there. I'll come and find you the second the scientists are done with him."

"Crash?" Einarr frowned.

Frey couldn't help but smile. "He means you should get some sleep while you can so that you'll be ready to deal with Aki when he wakes up."

Einarr's blue gaze rested on her, and she wished she hadn't opened her mouth.

"I will rest." His hand shot out and caught her elbow. "But I insist you accompany me."

Frey glanced at Brown. "Don't I have to be locked up some-where or something?"

"No, you're good. Less manpower if you're together."

She narrowed her eyes at him "Thanks a lot, Brown."

He winked as he opened the door into the room. "Always happy to aid young lovers."

The door shut behind her and she turned and walked straight into a two hundred and thirty pound wall of steel. Her nose bumped hard against Einarr's chest and she took an invol-untarily step backward, ending up plastered against the door.

Einarr stared down at her. "Do not *ever* do that again."

"What?"

"Put yourself in danger for my sake."

She scowled right back at him. "*Right,* like I'm going to let you die in front of me while I wring my hands and cry like a baby."

"Aki would not have hurt me."

"Didn't look like it from where I was standing. It's always

better to be safe than sorry." She shoved at his chest, and he rocked on his heels. "Now back off."

He rested one hand on the door behind her head. "I do not doubt your courage, Frey. But like all men, I would prefer my womenfolk to be safe and far away from the fighting."

"*Womenfolk?* So you can run around being all heroic and die rather than accept that a woman can fight alongside you?"

'You told me you wanted my protection," he growled.

"Not when you're the one whose about to die." She pushed him again. "Let me pass you male chauvinist pig."

This time he took a reluctant step back, and she ducked under his raised arm and got away. Of course, being as they were stuck in the same room, she didn't have many options. She headed for the small bathroom and slammed the door as hard as she could.

After using the facilities and splashing water on her face, she stared at her reflection in the mirror. There was no way out. Either she stayed in the bathroom until Einarr was called to his brother, or she went out to him and…what? She had nothing to apologize for.

A knock sounded on the door and she stiffened.

"What?"

"May I come in?"

She sighed and straightened up. "I suppose so."

He opened the door, which she'd forgotten to lock during all her flouncing, and came to stand behind her, his blue eyes meeting hers in the large mirror.

"I have never seen my reflection so clearly," he murmured.

"It's just a mirror." Frey said. His hands remained on her shoulders as he kissed the top of her head, which fitted, neatly under his chin.

"It is not made of polished metal."

"No, it's a kind of glass." She thought about moving away. The sensation of his fingers kneading the tight muscles of her shoulders kept her glued in place and in danger of purring like a cat.

"I should not have shouted at you." Einarr said quietly. "You did what any valiant warrior would do for a brother-in-arms."

"I'm not your brother." The moment she heard the words Frey rushed to take them back. "I mean you're welcome. And you're right I would've done that for anyone."

He continued to stare at her reflection in the mirror. "For anyone? It is strange because I would never even think of berating one of my fellow warriors for defending me. I would expect it as my right."

Frey smiled sweetly. "That's because you are a four-thousand-year-old sexist Viking pig. Or in simpler terms an old boar. I bet if a woman had done that in your time, you would've taken her over your knee and beaten her."

"Nay, we had shield maidens who fought alongside us."

"You did?" She frowned at him. "Then why are you so mad at me?"

He bit her throat and she shuddered. "Because you are mine, and I cannot bear to lose you."

"That's—"

He bit her again, this time more roughly. "You are *mine*."

"I can't be yours, you know that," she whispered.

"It is not something you or I can decide, Frey. We were fated to meet by the Gods."

"No, it was just luck." She swallowed hard. "Einarr, *look* at me. I'm just a boring old scientist who happened to be the first woman you saw when you woke up. Your feelings for me are awesome and all that, but they are *not* real."

He wrapped one arm around her hips and drew her ass tight against the hardness of his cock. "What I feel for you is quite real."

"That's just lust. You can't—"

She gasped as he sank his teeth into her shoulder and started unbuttoning her uniform. His large hands making short work of her tunic and bra, baring her breasts to his gaze. He cupped her breasts, his thumbs rubbing her nipples into two hard points. She arched her back and he groaned taking the opportunity to shove the rest of her clothes down to the floor where she automatically stepped out of them.

"Mine," he murmured. "*My* woman."

Being naked and in front of a mirror had never been her favorite place to be, but with Einarr's big callused hands roaming over her flesh, she almost didn't care. His cock pushed hard against the leather of his crotch making her writhe against him. He reached down and put his hand behind her knee, bringing it up to the countertop and set her foot down exposing her sex to his gaze.

His palm cupped her sex. "*Mine.*"

Using two fingers, he rubbed back and forth over her clit and then lower until she was shuddering and wet. He didn't stop, his thumb working the moisture around her now throbbing clit and then inside her in an endless and remorseless pattern. She climaxed, the sensation so tight and hard that she cried out, echoing his satisfied growl.

She could see everything he was doing to her in the mirror, her dark red swollen clit and the wet slippery opening to her sex where he stabbed his thumb deep.

"Please..." she whispered straining against him, pressing her ass against the unyielding stiff column of his cock. " Please fuck me."

"Not yet."

She reached back and dug her fingernails into his exposed arm. "*Please.*"

He used his fingers to spread her pussy lips wide and pressed his long middle finger inside her. It wasn't enough and he damn well knew it.

"Fuck me." This time she didn't beg, she demanded.

EINARR STARED at Frey's exposed body, the slick wetness on his fingers and the throb of her need playing out beneath his palm. For the first time in his life, he wished he had two cocks to ram into her and fill her until she screamed.

"Your sister has two men in her bed, aye?"

"Yes, but, what's that got to do with—"

"Do they fuck her together?"

"Yes."

"I wish there were two of me to fuck you right now, although I fear you might not survive it."

She glared at him in the mirror, her brown eyes flashing sparks like a fire. "I can take anything you want to give me. I'm a Pavlovan. We're built to deal with two mates."

He couldn't help but slide three fingers in and out of her wetness, aware how wide she was, and how much he wanted her. Her hand gentled on his arm.

"It's okay. I won't break. I promise you."

With a growl he released his cock and lifted her high. Both of them watched as he slowly lowered her onto his big needy rod. She took him easily and it was like coming home. After watching her risk her life for him, he wanted to be slow and tender to show his gratitude, but he couldn't do it. He had to possess her, to make her realize how much she needed him, to make her scream so hard that she'd never want him to stop fucking her.

She came suddenly around his thrusting shaft, each squeeze bringing him closer to his own climax, but he kept moving, pushing her onward, linking his mind to hers so that she'd somehow realize how restrained he was actually being.

"I know you're still mad but you won't hurt me. You couldn't."

Her thought reverberated through his mind, the stark truth of it making him wild. His hips pistoned back and forth as he fucked her with his full length, each stroke from root to tip, her body taking him, endlessly offering him sanctuary and fulfillment and...Gods...

With one last slam of his hips he pushed deep and held still as his come jetted out in rapid hot spurts. She climaxed with him drawing every last drop of seed from his thrusting cock. His chin came to rest on her shoulder and he opened his eyes and met her gaze in the mirror.

"It is not that I think you lack worth as a fighter, Frey, or wish to keep you doing woman's work. It is more that I fear I cannot protect you in this strange world—that you will be injured and I will not be able to save you."

She swallowed hard. "Which is exactly how I feel about you."

The corner of his mouth kicked up. "Then perhaps we are both fools?"

"For wanting to save each other? I suppose we are." Frey sighed. "But this can't last. I have to go back to Pavlovan, and you will be here for a long time in the rehabilitation center."

He eased his cock free and gently set her foot down on the floor. "I cannot accept this."

"You *have* to. I'm trying to be honest with you. There isn't another choice."

"That is not true." He moved away from her and she crossed her arms over her breasts. He washed and dried himself off, aware of her withdrawing from him in her mind as well as her body. "You simply do not choose to believe."

"That's not *fair*—"

"When the Gods and the Fates align we can do nothing but accept their wishes and sometimes find joy in them."

She raised her chin. "That's all very nice, but I don't believe in your Gods, and I know from personal experience that meeting someone and wanting them like *this* isn't good or sustainable!"

"You have left another man for this reason?" The thought of her with another man made him even angrier.

"No. My father did it to my mother."

"So you will leave me before I can leave you?" He raised an eyebrow. "I am not going anywhere, Frey. I am stuck in this Godforsaken world whether I like it or not and so are you." He turned to the door. "If Aki awakens I will go to him alone."

"Einarr…"

BEFORE FREY COULD SAY anything more, he bowed and walked out into the bedroom, closing the door quietly behind him. She stomped over to turn on the shower. What the *heeze* did he know? She wasn't some miracle worker or the kind of person who dreamed impossible things. Life had taught her that such optimism usually ended in heartbreak. Her dad had been a dreamer, and his romantic notions had left her family broken and bewildered.

She was practical, loyal and reliable. Maybe even a little boring. All qualities her father had lacked. She'd spent her whole life trying to make up to her mother for her father's desertion. She'd caused no trouble and tried to be the most perfect daughter imaginable. Believing she could have a chance with someone like Einarr was ridiculous and terrifying and…

"Dammit!" Frey thumped the tiled wall of the shower. "It's not *fair*."

He thought she lacked courage.

Even worse, he was probably right.

10

"Viking?" Brown knocked on the door. "Your brother is awake."

"Thank you," Einarr called out.

After a swift glance at the still closed bathroom door, he tapped in the security codes Frey had created and exited the room into the hallway beyond. In truth, he was glad to escape. His frustration with Frey's insistence that he could not be with her had made him pace the small space and contemplate punching a hole in the wall.

Brown stood guard by Aki's open door, his weapon at the ready. "You can go in. Behave yourself."

Einarr gave Brown a scathing look, took a deep breath and walked through the door. Aki was strapped to the bed but he was stirring and starting to mumble. Einarr came to stand by his head.

"Aki?"

His twin's blue eyes opened and blinked slowly. "Einarr? Are we truly with the Gods?"

"Not quite." Einarr put his hand on Aki's shoulder. "We were frozen in the ice for many years and were recently found and released."

"That makes no sense. When I woke up I was trapped in a metal box that rampaged through the blackness of the night sky."

"So was I. We were asleep for a very long time, Aki. Things have changed beyond our comprehension. Ships are built to fly between different worlds rather than just through the sea."

"I cannot believe this." Aki muttered. "It is a cruel joke played by the Gods. We are either dead or still dreaming."

"At first, I thought the same, but I've come to realize I am simply alive in a very different time. " Einarr patted his brother's shoulder. "I can't say I understand it yet, but if I am not to go mad, I will have to try. I wish you to try as well. These people are not our enemies Aki."

"Then why am I a prisoner?"

"Because you attacked the crew on the ship that brought you here."

"I had no choice. They attacked me when I came out of the ice. I'm not a coward."

"Neither am I."

"Then how is it that you speak so eloquently on their behalf?" Aki demanded. "Have they bewitched you?"

An image of Frey burned through Einarr's memory, and he pushed it aside. "Nay. I have just been awake for longer than you have and I have learned more. These people are not our enemies. They truly wish to help us."

"Then tell them to take us home."

Einarr sighed. "There is no 'home.' That world has gone."

Aki blinked up at him and shook his head. "I cannot accept that."

"If you give them your word of honor that you will not fight, I'm sure you'll be allowed to get up."

"And do what, Einarr? All I want is for things to get back to how they were."

Einarr offered his brother a drink of water and pressed the red button beside the bed to call the healer. To his relief Pel Aziz came through the door, her expression relieved as she studied Aki.

"I'm so glad you have regained consciousness, Aki, how are you feeling?"

Aki glanced at Einarr. "How is it that I can understand what she is saying now? I couldn't understand anyone on the ship. Is it more magic?"

"It is like magic." Einarr showed him the patch on his skin. "But it is also very useful, so please do not take it off."

"*We also have this.*" Aki spoke in his head. "*No one else can hear us here.*"

Aziz repeated her question, and Aki finally looked at her.

"Who are you?"

"I am a medical doctor and research scientist. My name is Doctor Pel Aziz. I'm here to take care of you."

Aki's eyes widened. "You can understand me?"

"Yes."

"Then release me from my bonds."

"You sound just like your brother," Aziz murmured as she ran a scanner over Aki's body. "You also seem to be in good shape. A little malnourished, but that's to be expected considering your past history." She took his hand and he tried to pull it back. "It's okay. I won't hurt you."

"As if you could, woman."

Aziz raised her chin and stared right into Aki's eyes. "Try me. I'm quite capable of defending myself."

Einarr cleared his throat. "Do not fight her. She is a healer."

"And obviously a warrior," Aki murmured. "I will remember that."

After a few puzzled minutes while the doctor tapped away at her white tablet, Einarr worked out how to raise the bed.

"May I release my brother now?"

Aziz looked up. "You'll have to check with Brown. He's in charge of security now."

Einarr glanced over at the door where Brown stood guard and raised an eyebrow.

Brown nodded. "You are both free to move around the medical facility but no further. You will also be accompanied by security personnel of my choosing and will be monitored at all times. Do either of you have a problem with that?"

"No, we do not." Einarr answered for both of them before Aki started to disagree.

"You will also be required to cooperate with both the FREN and TSA personnel who wish to speak with you both as soon as Aki is cleared by medical."

"I understand."

Einarr started undoing the straps that bound his brother to the bed. He didn't like having to obey Brown's orders but he had no choice. Until he discovered exactly what was required of him and his brother, he would continue to cooperate. For the first time in his life he had no purpose. He would have to find one soon or go mad.

Dr. Aziz talked with Brown before disappearing out the door promising to send food. Aki sat up; grimacing down at the blue gown he'd been dressed in and stretched his arms over his head.

"Where are my clothes and weapons?"

Einarr checked the cupboard and found his brother's garments neatly folded next to his sword and dagger. He handed over the clothing, aware of Brown stepping out into the corridor and closing the door behind him. He knew the man wouldn't go any further. But at least he was attempting to give them some privacy. Not that he could assuage his brother's fears or make anything right for him.

He hated that.

Aki placed his sword on the table and buckled his dagger into place at his hip. He finger combed through his long blond hair and re-braided it. He had always been more vain and careful of his appearance than his twin. He'd also been Einarr's protector and had more of a temper.

A knock at the door heralded the arrival of a veritable feast, including some kind of ale and thick slabs of roasted meat. It was easy enough for Einarr to sit opposite Aki and eat his fill, prolonging the moment when he would have to disappoint his brother and disclose his inability to change anything about their current predicament. He'd been so caught up with meeting Frey that he'd tried not to think about the future. As long as she was with him, he'd instinctively believed that everything would be all right.

But she didn't want to be with him. She didn't believe he meant what he said… she thought him infatuated or…

Was she right? Was his fear of dealing with the new world making him cling to her like a suckling child to its mother?

"Einarr?"

He jerked his attention back to his brother who was watching him intently.

"What?"

"Are you certain we are alive?"

"I'm afraid that we are."

"And we are in the future?"

"About four thousand years or so, aye."

Aki's blue eyes widened. "It is impossible."

"I agree, but it is true."

"And we can't get home?"

"Home as we know it no longer exists."

Aki sat down with a thump. "Our whole world has gone?"

"No, our 'planet' is still there, but it would be unrecognizable to you and me." Einarr knew he was being too short with his brother, but there was no point in pretending anything would change.

Aki put down his cup of ale. "Then what in Odin's name are we supposed to do now?"

"That, my twin is a very good question." Einarr tried to shrug off his own concerns. "I suspect the people from FREN and TSA might want something from us. I am not yet sure what that might be. I suggest we keep our counsel and listen to what they have to say before we make any decisions as to our future."

FREY DRESSED in the clean uniform she'd found laid out for her on the bed and wondered what to do next. Should she go and find the FREN rep and ask permission to leave the planet, or was she supposed to hang around waiting to be dismissed or court-marshaled?

"Tecky?"

"Yes, Slavin?"

"Are you okay?"

"As okay as anyone facing an ignominious dismissal can be, why?"

"I wanted to let you know that I contacted my cousin back in Pavlovan about what's been happening with you and FREN. He's on the council. He was most concerned and said he'd make sure your Pavlovan interests were properly represented."

"What exactly does that mean?"

"I'm not sure, but I hope he'll stop you from being prosecuted for something that wasn't really your fault. You can't choose who you are mated with."

"Perhaps you should also tell him about the other science officer on Aki's ship. He's Pavlovan too, and experienced a very similar situation *to mine—apart from the kissing bits. I wouldn't be surprised if he was dismissed or prosecuted by FREN as well."*

"Having two witnesses should help your case. I'll let my cousin know about this as soon as possible. When are you due to speak to the FREN rep next?"

"I've no idea. I assume they'll be more interested in interviewing the Bloodaxe twins than me."

There was a slight hesitation. "Have you seen Einarr's twin yet?"

"Nope. I don't think there's any reason for me to do so, is there?"

"I can sense him better than Einarr."

"That's weird."

"I know." Again that pause. "I'll let you know if my cousin has any definite plans in place."

"Thanks."

Frey brushed her hair into a neat ponytail and turned the collar of her uniform up to hide the bite marks Einarr had left on her shoulder. Her unremarkable face looked back at her from the mirror, and for a moment, she wished for some of Slavin's blond beauty. Einarr hadn't even glanced at Slavin, even though she was a telepath. But what if he'd met her first?

"And why are you trying to deny what you feel for your mate?" She asked herself loudly, her voice ringing around the tiled bathroom. "Why are you such a wuss?"

She turned away from her reflection in despair. Why couldn't the Gods have offered her a nice safe Pavlovan male rather than a four-thousand-year-old magical Viking? And what happened if one couldn't or wouldn't accept a mate? Would the Pavlovan Oracle offer her another one? Somehow she doubted it...

She wished she could talk to the Oracle right now. She was so conflicted.

"Tecky?"

A knock on the outside door made her straighten up and

walk out of the bathroom. She tapped in the codes and the door swung open to reveal Moshe, one of the security team from the ship. He appeared to have recovered from his encounter with Einarr.

He pointed at the door across the corridor. "Einarr's in there with his twin and the reps from TSA and FREN He asked if you could join him."

"Do I have to?"

Wow, she sounded like a whiny child. Having to see Einarr again made the idea of walking away from him even harder.

"I think he'd appreciate the support," Brown said quietly from his position outside the door.

And then Frey felt like a heel for even attempting to avoid her mate. If she was going to abandon him, she could at least support him right up until the end. Squaring her shoulders, she allowed Brown to open the door and went inside. The smell of roasting meat made her stomach rumble and she clutched a hand over it.

Gron, the TSA rep stood and bowed to her. "Science Officer Frey."

Mitzi Lahm stayed where she was and kept ogling the Vikings. Frey saluted, her gaze drawn to the opposite side of the table where the brothers sat side by side. They were identical in size, both had pale blue eyes, bulging muscles and fierce expressions. The only difference she could see was that Aki was blond and Einarr was dark. The other thing she noticed was that Aki's mind didn't call out to her.

"My lady." Einarr also stood. "May I make my brother known to you? Aki, this is Frey. She is the reason I didn't go mad when I woke up on the space ship."

"It's a pleasure to meet you, Aki." Frey risked a small smile at the blond Viking. "I apologize for jumping on your back and knocking you out."

"Ah, that was you, was it?" Aki's gaze became considering. "The women in this world are all warriors, then?"

"Most of them," Einarr answered for her. "They don't seem to believe they need a man, either." His cool gaze flicked over her and his mind remained closed. That hurt more than she had anticipated.

Aki laughed. "All women need a man. How else would they have children?"

Frey glared at him. "They don't need a man for that. Just his sperm."

Aki's gaze widened. "But, how—"

Einarr talked over him. "I was recounting the tale of my emergence from the ice to Gron and Mitzi Lahm. I thought you might wish to tell them what you witnessed as well, Frey."

Mitzi swiveled in her seat to stare at Frey. "We already have her report. Her participation isn't necessary."

Gron held up his hand. "I don't agree. I'd like to hear from Science Officer Frey."

Mitzi snorted and folded her arms shoving her ample chest upward drawing Aki's appreciative gaze. "Fine, but as far as FREN is concerned, she's already lost her job. I won't be recommending her to any other space program."

Frey set her jaw as she took the seat Gron offered her. "Have you both read the report from the science officer on Aki's ship? He noted the same sequence of events that I did. It can hardly be a coincidence that both Vikings defrosted at exactly the same time during the same phase of the eclipse."

Gron nodded. "She does have a point, Mitzi."

"But the other science officer didn't fornicate with his charge, did he?" Mitzi said sweetly.

"He was the first to be knocked out. Maybe he didn't have a chance to make the same physical connection I did." Frey said.

"As if a big strong Viking warrior would be attracted to another man," Mitzi scoffed.

"Why would he not?" Aki shrugged. "I am willing to enjoy a tumble in the hay with anyone." He met Frey's eyes and smiled slightly. "I can see why my brother was enticed into your bed. I would have done the same as he did."

Frey's cheek heated. "Thanks, I think." She didn't dare look at Einarr.

"Still—" Mitzi started up and Gron talked over her.

"Unfortunately, both the TSA and FREN have rules about fraternization with other crew members, rules which you broke, Science Officer Frey."

"Einarr wasn't a crew member."

"He was the property of FREN." Mitzi snapped. "And you had no right to act in such an unprofessional manner."

Einarr scowled. "I am nobody's property and neither is my brother. Frey and I had no choice in our joining. We were destined to meet by Fate. I do not regret my mating with her. She is my female."

"She can't be," Gron said gently. "You're still in a state of shock. Any decisions you make at this point are not really valid or realistic."

Einarr's laugh was harsh. "You sound like Frey. She too imagines I am not a man of my word."

Frey swallowed hard. "That's not true. I—"

Aki's voice sounded in her head as Mitzi interrupted her and went off on another rant. *"You are mated to my brother?"*

"I don't know."

"I can feel the link between you. It is strong."

"And there's nothing I can do about it. I'm about to lose my job and be sent away. Einarr will stay here with you."

"A warrior such as yourself does not fight for what she wants?"

"I'm a scientist, not a warrior."

"You do not care for my brother?"

"I—" Frey broke off contact as she noticed Einarr staring right at her. She returned her attention to Mitzi and Gron and

answered all the questions they threw at her. Despite being pressed, she couldn't bring herself to deny her sexual relationship with Einarr, or even to say it had been a mistake. And that lack of remorse would be her downfall. No one in the TSA or FREN would let her near another scientific mission in case she made a habit of seducing attractive aliens.

Eventually Gron nodded at the Vikings. "Thank you for all your help. We would appreciate your cooperation and your patience while we assemble a program to help you readjust to life in this century. We weren't anticipating the speed of your emergence from the ice."

Einarr pushed his chair back and looked up at Gron. "We will bide here as you wish. Unless you have the ability to magic us back to our original time, then I fear we are stuck on this planet and at your mercy."

"I repeat that we wish you no harm," Gron said earnestly. "After a period of necessary adjustment, we will do everything in our power to make sure that you both live full and satisfying lives."

"And what will you require from us in return?" Einarr asked.

"Your cooperation." Gron repeated.

"And your agreement to be studied by our scientists." Mitzi added. "We need to learn as much about your DNA as we can."

Aki snorted. "I do not understand these words."

"What she means is that you will be given everything necessary to survive and thrive in this world." Seeing the incomprehension of the men's faces, Frey couldn't help but speak up. "In return, you will help the scientists, the seekers of knowledge, and the healers find out more about you and how you are different to the current population."

"Studied as one would study an enemy's habits before moving in for the kill? Or as one hunts one's prey?" Einarr murmured. "Does this mean we will never be truly free?"

Frey looked at Gron and Mitzi. "That's up to them. I would

hope that you are eventually rehabilitated completely into society."

Mitzi stood and smiled at the Vikings before turning to Frey. "Perhaps we should leave the brothers to think through this discussion. Science Officer Frey, you will accompany me."

As Einarr made no effort to detain her, Frey could only walk out of the door and wait for Mitzi and Gron to come after her. Would this be the last time she saw Einarr? Could she even bear to have to see him again? It already felt like her heart was breaking in two.

Mitzi beckoned imperiously at the security guard. "Brown? Take Science Officer Frey back to the detention center."

"What have I done now?" Frey blinked as Brown approached her, his expression resolute.

"You are not a good influence on our guests, and you are still facing charges of dereliction of duty and fraternizing with an unknown alien race."

"He's *human!*" Frey snapped.

Mitzi ignored her impassioned interruption. "You will be tried, and if I have my way, your mind will be wiped before you are allowed back into a society far away from these Vikings."

"You can't do that to a Pavlovan," Frey raised her voice as Mitzi turned away and Gron followed her without even protesting.

Brown touched her shoulder. "Come on, Tecky. I have my orders."

"No!" Frey shrugged off his hand. "This can't be allowed to happen, I have rights, I want to see my—"

A hand clamped down hard on her shoulder. "There's no point in upsetting our guests now is there? Come on, or I'll get Dr. Aziz to knock you out."

Frey refused to stop struggling. Voluntarily leaving Alpha Three and the man she knew was her mate was one thing. Having those memories forcibly removed from her head was another thing entirely. She would not allow them to take that away from her, she would *not*.

She kicked out and caught one of the security guards in the kneecap and then knew no more as a needle jabbed into her neck and the whole world went black.

EINARR STARED down at his folded hands as Frey and the others left the room. He'd successfully managed to build a wall in his mind to keep Frey out, but it was a pitiful harsh existence being barricaded away from her warmth.

"Your woman is very beautiful." Aki said.

"She is not my woman. She does not want me."

"How can she not want you when your thoughts and hers are even more entangled than yours are with mine? She cannot break those bonds. She cannot deny them."

"She thinks I am clinging to her because she was the first woman I saw when I woke up and that when I grow accustomed to living in this strange world, I will no longer desire her."

Aki stretched and yawned. "Now why would she say that?"

"Because she thinks it is the truth?" Einarr growled. "And mayhap she is right."

"You don't really believe that, do you?" Aki considered him. "Perhaps she is trying to save you from yourself."

"Save me from a woman who isn't afraid of my strength or my magic?" Einarr shook his head. "Frey *is* my perfect woman. She just doesn't believe it."

"Then how are you going to convince her to stay?"

"You make it sound so simple." Einarr shot to his feet and took a turn around the room. "You have seen how the women are in this place. They cannot be told what to do like slaves."

"Perhaps you could make a bargain with the FREN and TSA

people. You will help with their studies if they let Frey stay with you."

"And trap her in a cage, too?"

"Bjáni!" Aki threw up his hands. "Then you both insist on being heroic and losing each other forever? If that is the truth, then you are a pair of fools." His expression changed as Einarr went still. "What is it?"

"I cannot sense Frey in my head."

"But we just saw her." Aki rose to his feet as Einarr charged toward the door, his axe already in his hand. "Where are you going?"

"To find her." Einarr wrenched open the door, and was met with a wall of guards all with their weapons raised and pointed at him. He recognized one of the men from the ship.

"Moshe, I wish you no harm. Where is Frey?"

"Brown's taken her to the detention center."

"What exactly does that mean?"

Moshe dropped his gaze and fiddled with his weapon. "She refused to cooperate with the FREN representative. They will keep her locked up until her trial tomorrow."

"Her *trial?*" Einarr realized he was shouting but he didn't care. "What in Thor's name is she supposed to have done?"

Moshe met his gaze, his expression neutral. "She will be charged with disobeying direct orders from her TSA superiors and from FREN."

Einarr's hand clenched around the handle of his axe. "What will happen to her if she is found guilty?"

"It depends on the judge coming in tomorrow. They are drawn from all the planets in the Trios System. She should be okay if she doesn't get an Etruscan. They *hate* telepaths and—"

"Moshe? May I suggest you shut the fuck up right now?" Brown appeared behind the group of guards who parted to let him through to confront Einarr. "Science Officer Frey will be fine, Viking. She resisted arrest and had to be temporarily subdued."

"If you hurt her I will kill you." Einarr glared at Brown. "You will take me to her immediately."

"I can't do that, pal." Brown sighed. "And if you attempt to get to her using excessive force, I've been authorized to knock you and your brother out, too."

There was a light touch on Einarr's arm. "Brother? Perhaps we should lower our weapons and consider what we wish to do next."

"I want to find Frey," Einarr growled. "There is nothing I wish to *consider.*"

Aki's grip tightened. *"We will help her better when they think we are resigned to her fate. Do not rush into this like a blundering ox."*

"You are giving me advice now?"

"Aye, because Frey's life matters to you more than anything. We cannot fail her."

Still holding Brown's unwavering stare, Einarr lowered his axe. "I wish to be present at her trial."

"I will ask if that is possible."

"Tell them that if I am not allowed to be present and Frey suffers from her association with me, I will not work with their scientists."

"And neither will I," Aki added.

"I'll tell them." Brown waited until Aki put his sword away and then gestured at the door. "Please return to your quarters. I'll keep you updated as to Science Officer Frey's condition and your request to be at the trial."

"Thank you, Brown."

"You are welcome, Viking." Brown waited until the guards had resumed their positions before escorting the brothers into their room. "Off the record, I don't believe this matter is being handled correctly. I'll do my best to stand as a friend to Tecky."

"I appreciate that." Einarr gave the other man an abrupt nod. "I will not allow her to be harmed."

"They won't kill her." Brown paused. "You can rest easy about that."

"Then what will they do?" Aki asked.

"The minimum, they'll strip her of her military and professional rank and drum her out of the scientific space corp." Brown shrugged. "She'll be allowed to return to her home planet, but her reputation will be in tatters."

"And what if the judge is an…" Aki looked at Einarr. "What was the word that guard used?"

"Etruscan." Einarr said.

Brown grimaced. "If the judge is Etruscan he'll probably try for a harsher sentence, including jail time."

"You are not reassuring me as to my mate's welfare, Brown," Einarr said. "I don't want her to suffer because of me."

"Maybe it's for the best." Brown said encouragingly. "You can't be imagining you have a future together or anything?"

Einarr swung around and barely resisted the impulse to wrap his fingers around Brown's neck and squeeze hard.

"She is *mine*."

"She's her own person, Viking. Women are no longer seen as possessions in this space system. And maybe, if she thinks it will leave you free of her, Tecky will be okay about taking her punishment. I know she wants you to stay here and transition into a normal life." Brown nodded at Aki and headed for the door. "I'll keep you both informed."

Einarr waited until the door shut, picked up the nearest object, and threw it hard against the wall where it shattered on impact. The shards of glass reminded him of the moment when he'd emerged from the ice and been reborn. He sank down onto his haunches and shoved his hands through his hair.

"I will not give her up, Aki."

"I understand." His twin patted his shoulder. "I have never seen you like this before Einarr."

"Brown is a fool, but he is also right. Frey *is* trying to protect me. That's why she keeps saying she doesn't want me."

"Then she is a noble and courageous woman."

"And a fool," Einarr exhaled. "By Thor, I don't mean that. Although I'd still like to shake her until her teeth rattle."

Aki grinned. "Then all we need to decide is how we are going to find her and set her free."

11

FREY SWAYED A LITTLE AS SHE FACED THE FRONT OF THE HASTILY convened courtroom. Her head still throbbed and she was queasy after her hurried breakfast. Because she'd attacked one of her guards the previous day, her hands were manacled behind her with a narrow plastic strip that bit into her skin. After a signal from the bench, Brown gently nudged her forward.

"Go on, Tecky."

She raised her chin and walked toward the central table, which faced the female judge who didn't look particularly warm and fluffy. In fact, her expression was downright hostile.

"She's Etruscan," Brown murmured in Frey's ear.

"*Frak.*" Frey breathed out the curse. "Preprogrammed to hate me on sight. I wonder if Mitzi arranged that?"

The man at the table to Frey's right stood and started speaking, introducing the judge, who went by the name of Trallis Verchon, himself as the FREN sponsored prosecutor and the male on Frey's left who was apparently her defense.

"Excuse me?" Frey said loudly. The man didn't stop speaking. "EXCUSE ME? I was not consulted about my defense. I wish to speak to the Pavlovan ambassador for this region."

The male stopped talking and glanced at the judge who stared at Frey.

"The Pavlovan ambassador has been informed of this trial. If he cannot be bothered to turn up, we are prepared to proceed without him."

"I am not prepared to do that," Frey said firmly. "I know my rights. Trios System regulations state that all officers of TSA are entitled to representation by a lawyer from their own planet."

"Orin, your representative *is* from Pavlovan."

"But I haven't had a chance to speak to him." Frey countered.

"He has been fully prepared by FREN to defend your case." The judge nodded at the two men. "Please proceed."

"But—"

"Science Officer Frey, if you don't keep quiet I will have you taken from the court and tried in your absence."

"You—"

"Be silent. This is your last warning."

Frey pressed her lips together as the prosecutor, whose name was Braze, began speaking. Hearing herself described as a sloppy worker who ignored protocol, disobeyed orders from superiors, and lacked basic human decency was difficult enough. When Braze started in on her morals, she had trouble keeping her temper. According to him, she was some kind of temptress who had deliberately led the poor little Viking astray and used him for her own wicked ends.

After this general character assassination, Braze moved on to specific incidents, and Frey's mind began to wander with the absurdity of it. She could only hope that Einarr and Aki had been kept in ignorance of her trial. The last thing she wanted was to be rescued by an irate Viking...

She glanced over at Braze, who was really warming up to his theme of her incompetence. All things considered, seeing Einarr bury his axe in the man's head might be quite cathartic. But she couldn't think about that now. Her yearning to be with her mate was hard enough to bear without asking him to commit murder for her. She had to believe that justice would be served. She had to believe the Etruscan judge would be fair minded and lenient.

Heeze… Frey sighed. Like that was going to happen. She was going down. The only question left was how severe would the penalty be?

Witnesses were called. To their credit, most of the crew from her ship tried hard not to implicate Frey. They were restricted to answering the very narrow questions Braze asked. All of which showed her in the worst possible light. If it was possible, the judge's lips narrowed even further making her look as if she was sucking on something sour.

Even Captain Travis tried to defend her in his own way, but Frey knew nothing would help. FREN wanted to hold her entirely responsible for their decision-making and there was nothing she or anyone else from the TSA could do about it. *Scapegoat,* was an Earth word. She wondered if Einarr knew it.

"Tecky?"

"Slavin. How are you?"

"I'm at the space dock with the Pavlovan ambassador. We're waiting for a member of the security council to arrive. We'll be with you as soon as we can."

Frey tried to relax as the prosecutor finally shut up and her defense stood. He consulted his notes and cleared his throat.

"The defense cannot dispute any of the evidence presented to the court so far. We do, however want to mention that until this incident, our client had an *exemplary* record and that in any sentencing, that record should be used to ameliorate the harshness of the punishment."

He sat down again.

Frey turned toward him. "That's *it?* That's all you have to say?"

"Science Officer Frey," the judge said. "You have been warned."

"But this is ridiculous!" Frey shouted as Brown advanced toward her. "He did nothing to defend me!"

The judge stood and looked right at Frey. "This court finds you guilty on all counts. You will be incarcerated in a class one Pavlovan penitentiary for a minimum of a year. Your memories of this entire incident will be eradicated. The court may rise."

"No!" Frey was yelling now as Brown dragged her toward the door of the court. "I refuse to accept this verdict. *Einarr, help me!*"

There was a sudden crash behind her and a scream and then Brown was knocked away from her. A huge muscled arm locked around her waist and dragged her back toward the wall. The plastic bonds around her wrists loosened as Einarr cut her free with his dagger.

"I am here, my female."

Amongst the screaming, she heard Trallis shouting orders. Aki came up behind the judge and held the tip of his sword to her throat. His blue eyes glittered as he smiled.

"Everyone get out, or I will kill her," he roared.

The legal teams took flight, followed by the remaining security guards leaving Aki, the judge, an unconscious Brown and her and Einarr occupying a suddenly quiet room.

"Are you unharmed, my heart?" Einarr demanded.

With a sob, Frey turned in his arms and buried her face against his armored chest. "I couldn't let them take my memories of you away. That's not fair. I have to have something left to remember you by."

"When you give me up?"

"I don't want to do that either, but I can't involve you in all this craziness. It's just not right."

He slid a finger under her chin and made her look up at him. "I am already involved. This entire world seems crazed to me.

Now that I have disrupted a court and taken a judge hostage, I suspect my chances of escaping your planet's justice have just shortened considerably. Mayhap we can share a cell?"

She gulped. "Oh Gods, *why* did you have to say that? It's so romantic."

"Frey, you called me from the ice. You saved my soul."

"I did what FREN told me to do. I didn't—"

He kissed her firmly on the mouth. "You called to my blood. We were fated to meet."

"But—"

Somewhere by her feet, Brown groaned and rolled onto his back.

"May I intrude?" Einarr's head snapped around toward the elegant white suited male who stood at the wrecked door. Frey gasped at the immense surge of telepathic power that radiated from the still figure. Behind him, stood Slavin and another man who both looked anxious.

"Senator *Ash?*" the judge whispered.

"Yes." The male's smile was charming. "I do hope I'm not interrupting anything." He glanced back at the door and beckoned Slavin and the man whom Frey reckoned had to be the Pavlovan ambassador forward. "My security team will make sure we aren't disturbed." He turned his attention toward Aki. "Perhaps you might lower your weapon and assist the Honorable Trallis Verchon to a seat?"

"Einarr?" Aki frowned and turned to his twin. "Shall I release this *Kúkalabbi?*"

Frey spoke fast. "This man is Senator Ash, the head of the Pavlovan Senate. He is the most powerful man on our planet."

"And a friend to you or our foe?" Einarr asked her.

"I would hope he's a friend." Frey noticed Slavin nodding vigorously.

"Then Aki, stand down and allow the judge to sit and speak with this man."

Frey held her breath as the senator took a seat opposite Trallis Verchon and waved at everyone else to do the same. Aki shook his head and stayed behind the judge, one hand on his sword as if ready to lope off her head at a word from Einarr.

Einarr took Frey's hand and sat beside her, his booted foot almost resting on Brown's head.

Ash looked down at the recumbent figure. "Perhaps Security Officer Brown might be helped into a chair as well."

With an ungracious sound, Einarr bent down hauled Brown to his feet and dumped him unceremoniously in a seat.

"Now, judge, would you be so kind as to repeat your verdict on this case to me?" Ash said.

"I found the prisoner guilty on all counts, Senator."

"And the sentence?"

Trallis raised her chin. "Science Officer Frey will be incarcerated in a class one Pavlovan penitentiary for a minimum of a year."

Frey turned to Ash when Trallis stopped speaking. "With all due respect, Senator. The judge forgot to mention the bit about eradicating my memory."

A slight crease appeared on Ash's smooth brow. "Are you quite sure she said that?"

Brown cleared his throat. "She did, Senator. I heard her. The court record should confirm it."

"You do realize, Judge Trallis that eradicating a telepath's memory is illegal?" Ash stated. "Amendment 3.275 to the Trios System Agreement states it quite clearly."

"I believe that amendment only refers to cases where the entire memory is removed, Senator Ash." Trallis managed to sound both contemptuous and smug. "I was instructed that only this particular event would be removed."

"No, that's not correct. Any memory eradication is illegal." He glanced over his shoulder at the Pavlovan ambassador. "You have the files on this don't you, Dracon?"

"I do, Senator and I will be quite happy to share them with the judge at her convenience."

Ash sat back slightly. "Then I think we can agree that the latter part of the sentence should be struck from the records, can't we Judge Trallis? You wouldn't wish your unfortunate lack of knowledge of your own star systems laws to become public, would you?"

Trallis glared at Ash, but did eventually nod. Frey breathed out hard through her nose.

"Now, as to the length of the incarceration…"

"Science Officer Frey's defense conceded that she was guilty of all charges," Trallis snapped. "I see no reason to revisit my decision."

Ash's faint smile died. "I will have to disagree with you. From all accounts, Science Officer Frey was defended by a man who didn't even attempt to get her side of the story or offer up any witnesses in her defense. If he had performed this most *basic* of tasks, he would have realized that Science Officer Frey has mitigating circumstances, which would have affected her sentence."

"I don't understand your point, Senator."

"It is quite simple. There is another amendment within the agreement that specifically addresses the individual cultural mating habits of all species in the Trios System."

"And what does that have to do with your science officer's inability to follow orders and her immoral conduct?"

"*Immoral?*" Ash raised an eyebrow and glanced over at Frey and Einarr who were still holding hands. "Ah, of course as you are not a telepath Judge Trallis, you would be unable to sense the complex bond that exists between mated couples."

The judge blinked. "You are suggesting that Science Officer Frey is *mated* to this Viking?"

"Aye." Einarr spoke up. "She is my female by right of blood and heart."

Ash turned to Frey. "Can you confirm that, Science Officer?"

She stared into Einarr's blue eyes and took a deep breath. "Yes. I believe Einarr Bloodaxe is my mate."

The expression of disgust on Judge Trallis's face was something to behold. "You expect me to take the word of a *telepath*? On my world, they aren't even given full citizenship."

Ash stood and inclined his head a frosty inch. "Not just the word of a telepath, Judge, but *my* word as the head of the Pavlovan Senate. They are not lying. I can clearly sense the bond between them. I am quite willing to swear that on oath in a court of law. If you don't adjust the sentence, I will personally ensure that the next thing you judge will be the annual wild hildabeasts contest out on Wraxon Five."

The judge subsided back into her chair, her face white. After a long moment, she looked up at Ash the set of her jaw rigid with fury. "I refuse to change my verdict. I choose to resign from this travesty of a court system."

"As you wish," Ash bowed. "We will arrange for a new trial for Science Officer Frey and erase all records of your ruling." As the judge rose to her feet, Ash continued talking. "You will also agree to keep this matter between us. If I hear any unsavory rumors about Science Officer Frey's reputation, I will pass all the information I have about you to the Trios System Legal Council. I'm sure they'll be in touch with you shortly afterward."

"Telepaths should never have been allowed into positions of authority," Trallis sneered. "Government becomes meaningless when run with emotion."

"You are entitled to your opinion, Trallis Verchon." Ash took a step to the side. "May I suggest you allow my ambassador to see you safely on your way to Etrusca before the two Vikings, who are also telepaths, decide to take justice into their own hands?"

With a last scathing look in Frey's direction, Trallis swept out of the room with the Pavlovan ambassador right on her heels.

"What an extremely unpleasant individual," Ash murmured. "I suspect the entire Trios System will rejoice at her unexpected retirement."

***

THERE WAS the sound of raised voices at the door. Even as Einarr stiffened, Brown went to see what was going on. He spoke over his shoulder to Ash.

"Senator, the representatives from FREN and the TSA wish to speak to you."

"I'm sure they do. Tell them to wait quietly, and I'll talk to them in a moment."

"Yes, sir."

Ash turned back to Einarr and Aki. "You are telepaths, aren't you?"

Einarr met his stare. "If by that you mean we can mind talk, then aye we are."

"Was it common in your day?"

"Nay, only a few families had the honor of being connected to our Gods with such magical powers."

"And how strange and miraculous is it that you come back to life and met a female who can read your mind as well?" Ash said softly.

"She called to me through the ice. I fought my way out to her."

"It also had something to do with the eclipse," Frey added, still flustered by the appearance of such a legendary telepath and the leader of the senate. "We're not quite sure how."

Ash nodded and slid a hand through his long, fair hair pushing it back over his shoulder. He looked tired. "When you and Aki feel ready to move on, you would be most welcome to reside on Pavlovan. We are always interested in meeting new telepaths and learning from each other. You both have such *interesting* minds."

Einarr nodded. "Your thoughts shine like the sun."

"You can sense me?" Ash smiled. "I am considered to be quite a powerful telepath." His expression sobered as he looked from Einarr to Frey. "If you wish to be together in the end, you might have to deal with some time apart in the present. Einarr needs to stay here with Aki to acclimatize to our world, and Science Officer Frey…"

"Is supposed to be going to prison," Frey muttered.

"I suspect house arrest for a period of weeks will be required," Ash finished after her. "I still need to speak to the FREN rep."

"She's after my blood, too."

"So I heard." Ash beckoned to Brown. "Let Gron and Mitzi Lahm in please."

"You know their names?"

Ash winked at Einarr, and for a moment, Einarr wondered what it would be like to share a bed with a man of such beauty and such power. "It took me quite a while to get here. I read up on everything my cousin Slavin sent me on the way."

He stood as Mitzi erupted into the room followed by Gron.

"Good morning."

Gron saluted. "Senator, I wish to offer you my apologies. When I heard the trial verdict, I realized that TSA protocol had been violated. I was already in communication with my superiors to overturn the sentence."

"So I heard, Gron." Ash paused. "It's a pity that you didn't think of that sooner, but I appreciate the effort and you may stand down."

Gron sank into a chair. Mitzi stared at Ash as if he were a god come to life. "You *are* here. It's true!" She pressed her hand to her bosom. "It is such a *pleasure* to finally *meet* you."

"Please take a seat." Ash waved her into a chair. "Judge Trallis has resigned and rescinded her verdict. We will conduct a new trial of Science Officer Frey."

"But—" Mitzi tried to laugh. "How can that be? She deserves to be punished. She—"

"Science Officer Frey found her mate and protected him to the best of her ability," Ash said firmly. "If you were a telepath, you would've done the same thing."

"I…would have?"

Einarr wanted to smile at Mitzi's confused expression, but Frey's grip on his hand was still so tight that he'd have her nails imprinted in his skin for days. Not that he minded—although he'd prefer her cat scratches on his back…

Beside him Aki snorted. *"Careful, brother. Guard your salacious thoughts. You have a room full of mind talkers around you."*

Frey's color rose even higher, and she determinedly wouldn't look at him or his twin.

Mitzi's gaze sharpened. "Are you suggesting that a Pavlovan finding their mate, if that is indeed what happened here, carries more weight than a crew member who disobeys or fabricates orders from their superiors?"

"I'm simply saying that it changes the nature of the perceived error."

Mitzi folded her arms. "I'm not willing to accept that."

"If that isn't a sufficient reason for you, then I'm sure FREN will be willing to publicly accept responsibility for their own failures during this mission."

"Hold up," Mitzi said. "What failures?"

Slavin stepped forward and handed Ash a white tablet, which he accepted with thanks. Behind Einarr, Aki stiffened. His gaze fixed on Slavin.

Ash glanced down at the tablet. "I have the highest security clearance possible in the Trios System. I recovered several top-secret security transmissions from FREN to the science officers on both ships. These messages confirm the orders both science officers insist they received and carried out with such disastrous effect during the eclipse. Orders that FREN denied sending in court today. "

Ash contemplated Mitzi's furious face. "If you don't believe the desire to find their mates made the Vikings emerge from the ice, then you have to believe that the orders from FREN to change the settings on the internal probes *within* the ice worked with the unknown effect of the eclipse to accelerate the defrosting process. I believe those codes were sent out by you, Mitzi." Ash held out the tablet. "Do you wish to see your messages?"

Mitzi audibly swallowed. "You…can't have accessed FREN channels. You aren't authorized."

"I am now." Ash met her gaze. "If you wish this information to remain private you must agree to accept a lesser sentence for Science Officer Frey."

Einarr could almost hear the frantic workings of Mitzi's mind as she scowled down at the tablet.

"All right!" she snapped. "I'll go along with this farce."

"Thank you." Ash retrieved the white tablet. "I will speak to the head of security on Alpha Three, FREN and the TSA and make certain that we are all agreed. Does anyone have any other questions?"

Mitzi stormed out, followed quickly by Gron and a grinning Brown, leaving Ash contemplating the Vikings. Frey finally let go of Einarr's hand and went over to the senator.

"Why?" she whispered. "Why did you do all this for me?"

His smile gentled. "Because no one should be deprived of his or her mate. I almost lost my female once, and I would not wish that on anyone." His mouth kicked up at the corner. "And, I owed my cousin Slavin a favor from when we were children. I'll leave it up to her as to whether she tells you what I did."

Aki bumped against Einarr's shoulder. *"I wonder if Ash would consider sharing our bed? I suspect he would make a worthy mate."*

Ash looked up and caught Aki's appreciative gaze. *"Alas, I am happily mated to both a male and a female who would not take kindly to my bedding you both—but if I was single...believe me I would be honored."*

His gaze fell on Slavin. *"Don't be too downhearted. I suspect my cousin would appreciate the opportunity to meet you, Aki."*

Without another word, Aki pushed past Einarr and converged on Slavin who clutched her tablet to her chest and stood her ground. A flash of something visceral passed between them, and Einarr discreetly raised the shields in his head.

He strolled toward Frey and nodded to Ash. "My thanks, Ash. I do not understand exactly what you did, but you vanquished my female's enemies and for that I am grateful."

"You are welcome, Einarr. Your mate will have to return to Pavlovan for a few weeks to serve out her sentence, but after that she will be free to visit you here and bring you home to Pavlovan if you are so inclined."

"You will allow me to leave Alpha Three?"

"If you wish to."

"Mitzi said I would have to stay here and be tested by your healers."

"Mitzi was wrong. After the initial rehabilitation sessions, you can go wherever you please."

"I will go where Frey is." Einarr glanced over his shoulder at Aki who was still talking intently to Slavin. "I suspect my brother will favor Pavlovan, too."

Ash bowed. "I will be leaving Alpha Three tomorrow morning. I will take Science Officer Frey into my custody. I suggest you make the most of your time together tonight."

Einarr went down on one knee and kissed Ash's hand. "I am your man for life, Ash. Yours to call, and yours to command. I pledge you my loyalty."

For a fleeting moment Ash's hand came to rest on his head. "I accept your oath, Einarr Bloodaxe."

Einarr stood, grabbed Frey's elbow and walked her toward the door. If she was leaving him tomorrow, he wanted to enjoy every last moment with her behind a closed door.

Frey allowed Einarr to lead her out of the courtroom and back down the hallway. As he seemed to know where he was going, she didn't argue, her mind still too busy trying to come to terms with what had happened. She'd heard Senator Ash was an exceptional man, but she hadn't expected him to turn out to be her own personal savior.

"Here." Einarr guided her through a door and shut it behind them. "Can you secure it against everyone?"

"Yes." She pressed her hand to the security panel and realigned the locks without really thinking and realized they were back in the room they'd shared before Aki had woken up.

Frey sank down on the side of the bed and closed her eyes as Einarr disappeared into the attached bathroom. She heard water running and then he was beside her again, kneeling on the floor, a cold cloth in his hands.

"Frey?"

She stared down at him. "I am so glad you are with me," she said simply. "When I realized that I might lose all knowledge of you, I..." she shook her head. " I realized how stupid I'd been, and how cowardly and—"

He put his finger on her lips. "You are no coward. You fought for me in your own way." He sighed. "I am the one who should be apologizing. I could not save you. If Ash hadn't arrived, the guards would probably have shot Aki and me, and you would be on your way to prison. But when you called out to me…despite everything, I could not stop myself from coming to your aid."

She reached down to cup his cheek. "And I couldn't stop calling out to you to save me. I realized I would rather die alongside you than be taken away to die alone."

He turned his face into her palm and kissed it. "Then we are both fools."

"I think we've already agreed that. Will you be okay? I mean all right when I'm in Pavlovan?"

He grimaced. "I will miss you greatly, but I will survive the separation if I know you will return to me."

"And what if you change your mind and realize I'm not the right person for you?" Frey took a deep breath. "We hardly know each other really, do we? And you might feel differently when you are more familiar with this world."

"Frey." He held her gaze. "I *know* you."

"Only for a couple of Earth weeks."

"*Weeks?* Don't you understand, my love? I've been waiting for you for *four thousand years.*"

"Oh," she breathed.

"I was barely aware when I was trapped in the ice. Sometimes, I felt a wisp of emotion, or a sense of *someone*, but when I felt you…" He let out a breath. "I had no choice, but to force myself back to life. For *you*…"

"I don't deserve such devotion. I'm just a plain boring old science officer with nothing in particular to be proud of." She paused. "Apart from the way I shouted down that judge at my trial, and when I saved you on the ship and—" She looked down at him. "Maybe I'm not such a wuss after all."

"I am not sure what a wuss is, but you are the bravest woman

I have ever met." He pressed a kiss to her knee. "May I make love to you? If we are to be apart, I wish to have good memories to keep me strong."

She opened her arms wide, and he came down over her, pushing her onto the mattress, his big solid body covering her entirely. With a soft sound, he drew her arms over her head and held them at the wrist in one easy grip.

"Will you think of me when you are at home?" He nudged her knees apart with his thigh and resumed his position between them, the hard ridge of his shaft now wedged against her sex.

"Yes."

He rocked his hips. "Will you dream of me?"

"*Yes.*"

He kissed her nose and then her forehead before making his way down to her mouth and possessing it. She responded immediately, her body aroused and her mind reaching out to his. This time she had no barriers or self-doubt. He was her other half, or was that her other third? And be dammed to all the problems they would undoubtedly face. They would meet them together.

He released her hands and started to undress her, placing kisses on each piece of skin he uncovered until she was rubbing against him and demanding more. When she was completely naked, he rose over her and stripped, throwing his clothes to the floor to join hers in an untidy heap. As she watched his strong body emerge, she shivered with need. His skin was scarred from battles long past and his muscles bulged and flexed as he moved. She raised a languid hand and traced the black pattern of the tattoo that ran up his left arm.

He lowered himself over her and she caught the scent of leather and the sea and moaned out loud as he licked her nipple into his mouth and caressed the other one between his finger and thumb.

"My woman."

His hand slid between her spread thighs and he murmured his pleasure as his fingers encountered her slick readiness.

"You want me."

There was a hint of dark satisfaction in his voice that didn't offend her at all. Despite being thrust into a completely new world, Einarr had known what he'd wanted from the first moment he'd seen her. One had to admire that in a man and especially in a life mate.

"Take me inside you, then."

The crown of his cock nudged her clit and then slid downward and inward filling her so completely that she sighed with pleasure and brought her legs high around his hips. He pushed deep and held still, the throb of his shaft mimicking the beat of his heart and the sensation of him inside her head.

She angled her hips, inviting him deeper, and then gasped as he started to pump harder, each thrust nailing her to the bed. She wrapped herself around him as tightly as she could absorbing his movements and opening herself up to him. His scent filled her nostrils and she licked his throat and then bit him, sending a shudder through his frame and increasing his frantic pace.

"Come for me."

His fingers slid between them and he stroked her clit with his callused thumb until she forgot everything but the pleasure and the need in a shattering climax. Even as she tried to relax, he cupped her ass in his big hands and angled her higher against the roll of his hips. Each stroke of his cock pounding against her clit until there was nothing but a thin blue light of ecstasy connecting and reforming them into one entity that could never be broken.

"Ah, by Odin..."

Einarr groaned against her throat and then came deep within her, each hot pulse setting off another climax for Frey and prolonging his release. He lowered himself over her and laid still, his heart pounding against her breast. Her hand remained tangled in his long black hair.

Silence enveloped them, and Frey let it consume her as her mind slowly and reluctantly detached itself from Einarr's. She sensed that even if they were apart, she would never be completely alone again. She'd always believed that would be terrifying.

It felt...wonderful.

EINARR ROLLED onto his back and stared up at the ceiling, aware that during their coupling he had somehow lost himself again, but gained so much more.

"You will come back to me," he said the words out loud rather than in his mind.

"Yes," Frey said. "I don't think I could stay away."

He drew her against his chest as a wave of thankfulness swept over him. The days ahead would be difficult, he had no doubt of that, but at least he would have Frey and Aki at his side. She nuzzled his chest.

"TSA law also states that if I go into a mating phase, then I have to be given leave to be with my mate or mates."

"What does that mean?"

"Every so often the female in a triad gets the urge to breed. She doesn't actually have to have a child, but the desire for her mates becomes paramount and it is their duty to serve her." She sighed. "That's why a lot of females end up with two males."

Einarr opened his eyes. "One man isn't sufficient to satisfy his woman?"

"Not during a mating phase. A man might have to work very hard if he ends up with two women."

Einarr considered that information. "I cannot decide which I would prefer. Two females to satisfy, or the prospect of competing with another male in my bed."

"You might be grateful to have him there." Her fingers spread out over his chest. "But the idea of a third doesn't bother you?"

"Why should it?"

"I thought Vikings became Christians."

"Most of them did. My family also kept up the old ways. We knew magic existed and we were unwilling to give up our traditions."

"That's good."

He kissed her hair. "Because you are already wishing for another man? Perhaps Aki—"

She slammed her hand over his mouth and came up on one elbow. "God, *no,* that would be far too weird. We can wait until we can both go before the Oracle of Pavlovan. Sometimes she will give you the name of your third. I think she would like to meet you anyway. She is a magical being." She hesitated. "My mother said the Oracle told her to call me Frey after the Nordic goddess. I wonder if she knew I would find you?"

"If she is a seer. Then I would imagine she did know. I would like to meet her."

"Then we shall go to the temple when you are free to leave here." She smiled down at him. "And I also think Aki is far too interested in my friend Slavin to want to share your bed."

"I noticed that."

"She is a wonderful person. He would be lucky to have her as a mate."

"As I am to have you." He reached across and lifted her over him so that she straddled his lap. "Now I am tired of talking, woman. Perhaps you might consider sitting on my cock and riding me?" He smiled into her beautiful flushed face. "I do have four thousand years of no fucking to make up for."

She squirmed against his stomach and then raised herself to take him deep. He held his breath as he slowly filled her.

"You hold my heart in your hands, Frey."

She sighed. "You do say the most romantic things."

"I mean them."

"I know." Her mouth trembled and a tear dripped down her cheek to land on his chest. "I just hope I can be worthy of you."

He hooked his hand around the back of her neck and brought her face down to his. She was his lodestone, his guiding star.

"Trust me. You already are."

The End

A NOTE TO READERS

Dear Readers,

Welcome to the science-fiction erotic romance world of the Triad System where telepaths roam, and forming a three-way partnership often has its ups and downs. In this particular adventure a four-thousand-year old Viking is being transported through space. Now what could possibly go wrong with that?

Major thanks to Kate Laity for the Old Norse translations!

If you enjoyed this book, please consider leaving a review at your favorite retailer.

If you want to read more of my books, please check out my website and consider joining my newsletter for the fastest updates and early contests to win new books.

katepearce.com/newsletter

164

Continue the series with VIKING CLAIMED...

Prologue

The Triad System

"Aki... you aren't even trying."

Aki looked across the room at his twin brother, Einarr. "Trying to what?"

"Learn."

Aki shoved back his chair and rose to his feet. "Because it doesn't interest me." He gazed longingly out of the window into the darkness of the strange planet he now inhabited. "I want to be outside. I want to go *home*."

Behind him his brother sighed in a way that had begun to infuriate Aki greatly.

"There is no home, you know that."

Aki swung around, his braided blond hair catching his

cheek. "How do you know? We could be bewitched. The Gods could be lying to us."

"For what purpose?" Einarr stretched out his long legs and tried to look relaxed, but Aki wasn't fooled. "You have seen the pictures. The Earth is completely changed beyond our wildest dreams."

"It could be a lie."

"Again I ask you why would anyone want to lie to us? We defrosted four thousand years too late. We should be grateful that these people have welcomed us into their world and are trying to help us even when you are being so pigheaded."

"I am not being pigheaded." Aki glared at his twin. "But then I am not the fool who thinks he's found his mate and *wants* all this to be true."

Einarr rose slowly to his feet, his blue eyes narrowed. "Are you questioning my honor, brother?"

Aki reached forward and poked Einarr's broad chest. "You won't even fight with me anymore. Your female has your cock in a stranglehold."

Einarr's gaze went stony. "My female is thousands of miles away on a different planet."

Aki pushed him again, making him rock back on his heels. "Is that why you are in such a foul mood?"

"At least I have a reason." Einarr shoved him back. "You, on the other hand, are just contrary. *Halfviti!*"

"*Kukalabbi!*" With a growl Aki launched himself at his brother. To his surprise, his challenge was met and accepted, and within seconds they were rolling around on the floor, desks and chairs and equipment falling around them as they tried to choke and punch the other into inglorious surrender.

An alarm blared somewhere, and Aki was pulled off his brother by two of the security team that accompanied them everywhere. Einarr looked up at him, his mouth bloody.

"As I said, you are a fool, a halfwit. The longer you take to complete this task, the longer we have to stay here on this Mitan moon. I want to go to Pavlovan."

Aki tried to shrug off Brown and Ilker, the two men who held his arms tightly behind his back. "You can get a female here."

The sound Einarr made was almost inhuman as he struggled against the guards. "I want *my* female. If you do not care who or what you fuck, Aki, stay here. I swear to the Gods that I will finish the tasks assigned to me and leave you behind." He glanced up at his guards. "You can let me go now. I will not touch him. I am done with him."

"Release him," Brown, the head of security spoke up.

Einarr stood, and after one last glare at Aki, walked out, slamming the door behind him.

Brown sighed as he surveyed the wrecked room. "Ross, keep an eye on Einarr and get someone here to clean up again." He dropped his hold on Aki's right arm. "And you'd better get a grip. Did you just call your twin a scumbag?" Brown tapped his earpiece. "That's the closest translation I could get. What the frak was that all about?"

"My brother is a lovesick fool."

"Your brother has completed his onworld training and is about to leave you here and go to another planet. Is that what you want?"

Aki shook off the second guard and swiped at his face. His nose appeared to be bleeding and two of his teeth felt loose. Experimentally, he cracked his jaw and winced.

"I want to go home."

"You won't be going anywhere if you don't pass Reintegration 101," Brown stated. "Our scientists would love that."

"What do you mean?" Aki turned to survey the chief of security who wasn't known for his sweetness of tongue or his inability to pull a punch.

"If you don't get with the program, FREN will be suggesting

you aren't capable of dealing with your new world and need to be closely watched by our scientists. You think you're in a cage now, mate, you wait until you see what they do to you."

Aki kicked a chair. "This 'work' you expect me to do makes no sense. It does not *test* me. I already know who and what I am. I am a *warrior*."

"You can be a warrior in the bloody Pavlovan army if you want, but you've still got to pass the tests."

"Brown, you bore me."

"Just trying to get the idea through your four-thousand-year-old thick skull." Brown headed for the door. "There are always wars to fight, Viking, you will still be needed, but—"

"First I have to pass the stupid tests," Aki finished for him.

"Do you want to go to the infirmary and get your jaw checked out?"

"It is fine."

Brown sighed. "Bloody stubborn Viking idiot."

Aki picked up one of the chairs and set it in front of the table with the white screen on it. He sat down and the screen came to life. The thought of any scientists getting near him and treating him like a worthless dog was enough to help him concentrate.

The voice in the box started speaking and for the first time, Aki sighed and paid attention.

End of Sample
To continue reading, be sure to pick up Viking Claimed at your favorite retailer.

The Sinners Club

Historical Erotic Romance

When intrigue collides with heated passion behind the closed doors of
the Sinners Club there is nowhere left to hide.

.

The Morgan Ranch Series

Contemporary Western Romance

A Northern Californian ranching family torn apart by tragedy
reluctantly return home to discover not everything was as they thought
it was, and that love, and forgiveness can sometimes go hand in hand.

.

The Millers of Morgan Valley Series

Contemporary Western Romance

When the mother you haven't seen for twenty years asks to visit your
family ranch and set the record straight, how will her ex and six adult
children react? The loves and sometimes messy lives of a ranching
family.

.

The Turner Brothers

Contemporary Erotic Western Romance

Three half-brothers find their own uniquely passionate ways to find
the loves of their lives and accept exactly who they are—no holds
barred.

.

The Obsidian Series

Sci-Fi Romance

Join a renegade band of telepaths roaming the galaxy to protect and rescue their race from the evil empire intent on destroying them.

.

Planet Valhalla Series

Sci-Fi/Futuristic Erotic Romance

One human female crash lands on a planet full of men descended from the Vikings, one of whom is the King who claims her as his mate— what could possibly go wrong? A sexy romp through the stars with excessive sex, a touch of humor and some very satisfied women…

.

The Triad Series

Sci-Fi/Futuristic Erotic Romance

Welcome to an imaginary world where civilizations, clash against the new and unknown, where telepaths are revered and reviled, and where your destiny can be preordained by a living oracle. Add in a group of super-soldier telepaths rescued from Earth and forming sexual triads for life becomes even more complex and life changing.

.

The Tribute Series

Sci-Fi/Futuristic *Dark* Erotic Romance

To save their planet from extinction the government will demand everything from the condemned few—willingly or not.

"Fans of no-holds-barred erotic portrayals of non- and quasi-consensual encounters will devour this steamy triptych."

– Publishers Weekly

Soul Justice Series

Paranormal Romance

Come and join a San Francisco based secret government department who investigate the monsters under the bed while risking their psychic abilities and even their own lives.

The Tudor Vampire Chronicles

Paranormal Historical Romance

Druids, Vampires and the court of King Henry VIII and his many wives form the backbone of this intriguing series as good fights evil through the first ever female Vampire slayer of her line, Rosalind Llewellyn.

Kurland St. Mary Mysteries

Historical Mystery

Writing as Catherine Lloyd

Join wounded cavalry hero Major Sir Robert Kurland and Lucy Harrington the rector's eldest daughter as they solve crimes in their quiet little village and gradually learn to appreciate each other.

ABOUT KATE PEARCE

New York Times and *USA Today* bestselling author Kate Pearce was born in England in the middle of a large family of girls and quickly found that her imagination was far more interesting than real life. After acquiring a degree in history and barely escaping from the British Civil Service alive, she moved to California and then to Hawaii with her kids and her husband and set about reinventing herself as a romance writer.

She is known for both her unconventional heroes and her joy at subverting romance clichés. In her spare time she self publishes science fiction erotic romance, historical romance, and whatever else she can imagine. You can find Kate at katepearce.com.

amazon.com/author/katepearce

goodreads.com/katepearce

bookbub.com/authors/kate-pearce

facebook.com/KatePearceAuthor

twitter.com/kate4queen